HER HIDDEN PAST

A ROSEMARY RUN THRILLER

KELLY UTT

Her Hidden Past is a work of fiction. Any references to historical events, real people, or real places are used fictitiously. Other names, characters, places, and events are products of the author's imagination, and any resemblance to actual events or places or persons, living or dead, is entirely coincidental.

2019 Standards of Starlight Paperback Edition

Copyright © 2019 by Kelly Utt-Grubb, writing as Kelly Utt

www.standardsofstarlight.com

ISBN: 978-1-7337712-5-2

Cover art by Justin Carolyne

PROLOGUE

One rainy September afternoon as Bea Hughes sat painting in her backyard art studio, the telephone rang. Its loud rattle made Bea startle. Hardly anyone called on the landline anymore. Bea knew that her elderly mother, Lana Denton, was seated near the phone in the living room reading the daily newspaper. Her son, Max was somewhere in the house, probably playing a video game or fiddling with his comic book collection. Since Bea was covered in acrylics and couldn't imagine who would call, she paused, hoping someone else would pick up the phone so she didn't have to.

When the ringing continued, Bea lurched for the receiver, accidentally knocking over her easel and splattering wet blues and greens all over her sandals. Exasperated, she feigned her nicest voice and said hello. She was, unfortunately, well-versed in the art of faking enthusiasm.

Bea couldn't be sure what she'd expected, but it certainly wasn't what she heard in response to her simple greeting. A robotic voice on the other end called Bea by her full name, Beatrice Elisabeth Hughes, then said the words which for years had haunted her nightmares. Words that would threaten to destroy Bea's family. Words that would seep angrily into her body and chill her down to the very bone.

"I know what you've done."

Bea's heart raced as she nervously twisted the coiled, black telephone cord around her fingertip. She felt like a child in trouble rather than an intelligent, capable woman in her thirties. She didn't dare say another word. *What could she say?*

Lowering the receiver under her chin and tilting her head over to secure it against her shoulder, Bea stepped towards the window and pulled back the floral-print curtains to look outside. She half-expected to see someone there, ready to forcibly take her away from her small-town life. If she was being honest with herself, she had half-expected that to happen for years. But no one appeared to be out there, save for Marmalade, the Hughes family's orange tabby cat who sat cursing the rain while huddled under a patio lounger.

Shaken but determined, Bea stood up as straight as she could and cleared her throat. She told herself she'd try to handle this head on. Even though she didn't feel like a capable adult, she willed herself to act as if she was one. Using a wrist, she brushed a few disobedient strands of dark, silky hair out of her eyes, then opened her mouth to speak.

Before she could say anything, she heard a faint clicking sound on the line.

"Are you still there?" Bea asked, hesitantly.

"Yes," the mechanical voice replied. "I said I know what you've done."

A louder click this time and the line went dead, blaring a forceful tone that could be heard even without holding an ear to the receiver.

Bea's heart nearly burst out of her chest as the realization settled over her. Not only had she been discovered by an unknown mystery caller, but someone inside her own home had picked up the phone. They had been listening in on the line.

1

W *hat next?* Bea thought as the telephone dangled in her outstretched hand, still sounding its incessant warning. A vintage clock sitting on a nearby project table ticked urgently, forcing its way into Bea's awareness and competing to be heard over the phone. Time was running out.

Back in the early days after the incident, Bea's fear of being caught had nearly consumed her. Max was a young boy then, barely in preschool. Bea had known she must hold it together. For Max. Her boy needed her desperately.

Bea's husband was a nice man and a cheerful father, but John Hughes didn't have what it takes to properly raise a child on his own. Besides, life in the public eye would have prevented him from putting the necessary time into child rearing. It was the exception rather than the rule for John to come home at a reasonable time in the evening. If Bea had been taken away, Max would have, no doubt, been raised by a nanny. The thought still made Bea shudder.

Perhaps it all would have been easier to take if the events leading up to the incident had been less dramatic. Bea knew she shouldn't have been there that night, especially since Max had been with her, his trusting eyes looking on as he leaned his little head on the side of his car seat. Even now, Bea could remember the scene as if it were right in front of her. She could feel the fog and the cool, damp air. She could smell the peanut butter and jelly sandwich she had hastily thrown together in case Max grew hungry, waiting in a brown paper bag within the console of her minivan. She could hear the chorus of bullfrogs as they did their best to ratchet up the volume on an already too-intense night.

The incident had been ten years prior. Bea should have tried harder to forget.

Standing still like a statue in her studio, she remained frozen in place. Her athletic legs felt useless and full of concrete. Her skin seemed taught as a turtle's shell, rigid and immovable. Mustering every ounce of her energy, she hung up the phone with a clank, then looked out the window again, expecting to see someone there this time.

Get it together, she told herself. She listened for signs of movement, but heard nothing except the gently falling rain.

Out of nowhere came a rapid series of knocks on the door. Bea's body grew even more rigid as her panic shifted into overdrive. She was certain this was it. *The end.* The caller who knew what she had done was out there. They had to be. *Who else?*

Feeling like a caged animal and suddenly wanting to flee, Bea's muscles kicked into gear. She paced back-and-forth in the small room. Her mind tumbled as she frantically searched for an escape route. Only there wasn't one. The studio had a single door and window, and both faced forward into the backyard towards the house. There was nowhere to run. Her only option might have been to remain perfectly still and quiet until the person who had knocked went away. For a moment, that's what Bea thought she would do. Like an ostrich with its head in the sand, she would hide and pretend this wasn't happening.

Another series of knocks came, louder this time. Bea's visitor was growing impatient.

Nauseous now and beginning to perspire, Bea picked up a handful of her largest paintbrushes and gripped them together like a knife. If she had to put up a fight, she reasoned, the paintbrushes were the only objects available which might assist her in defending herself. Bea thought about how she would go for the eyes right away. No point in waiting. If it meant her or them, Bea would give it all she had. She owed that much to Max. Even if not to John.

Growing furious and fueled by an instinct for self-preservation, Bea steeled herself. Whatever awaited her, she would face it right here and now. She had used violence once before and, in this moment, she realized she'd do it again if she had to.

Quickly, she flipped open the lock and pulled back the door, holding the makeshift knife high above her head.

"Bumble?" her sisters said in unison as they looked at Bea in disbelief. Bumble Bea had been an unfortunate childhood nickname her twin sisters refused to let go of.

Ruth took the lead. She always did.

"What do you think you're doing?" she asked.

"Yeah," Natalie echoed. "You look like you're ready to murder someone. In some kind of weird paint rage."

"Like Van Gogh," Ruth said in a mocking tone, finishing her twin sister's thought. "Bumble Bea, are you going to cut off an ear?"

The twins laughed knowingly as if they were still middle-school girls. In fact, Bea thought they looked like middle-school girls, giggling in the rain under matching plaid umbrellas. Their coordinating rubber boots completed their outfits.

Bea was two years younger and often the butt of her sisters' jokes. Thankfully, Ruth and Natalie lived in Sacramento now. Even though it was less than a two-hour drive, the pair seldom came home to Rosemary Run for a visit. Ruth was married with a couple of kids, while Natalie's life seemed to be in suspended animation, waiting to begin. It didn't help matters that the twins were joined at the hip. Bea had always figured that only so many men would go for such a setup. And, truth be told, she'd wondered why Ruth's husband, Steve Robeson, had. But who was Bea to judge? Her marriage to John was far from perfect.

"You two scared me," Bea said, the meek demeanor she exhibited around her big sisters taking over. Her change of disposition was probably a good thing. Bea knew she needed to calm down and think. "Is anyone else out there with you?"

"Just us," Natalie said. "Who were you expecting?"

Bea eased her head outside the studio door and looked around. Satisfied, she slowly lowered her hand and returned the paintbrushes to their resting spot on the easel. "Come in," she said. "You're getting all wet out there."

"Oh," Ruth responded without moving to enter the studio. "We were hoping we'd entice you to join us in the house. We were just there, having tea with Mom in the living room."

"Until the phone rang..." Natalie added coyly. Ruth jabbed her twin in the side with an elbow. Another inside joke for the two of them.

Bea's innards turned to mush as a fresh wave of nausea moved through her body. *Did they know?* She put an arm out to steady herself against the door frame. She could feel the color drain from her face.

"What is it, Bumble?" Ruth asked. "You look like you've seen a ghost."

Bea shook her head, trying to shake it off. "Nothing's wrong," she said in the most convincing voice she could manage. "I'm... fine."

"You sure about that?" Ruth pressed, peering into the studio. "It looks like you spilled some paint."

"Fine," Bea assured. "Tea with Mom sounds lovely. I'll just get my umbrella."

Bea closed the door behind her and leaned hard against it. She tilted her head back and looked up, willing herself to hold it together. She stayed like that for a few moments until the ceiling stopped spinning. Then she collected her umbrella, exited her studio, and followed her sisters through the back door of her house, stepping over Marmalade along the way.

"**E**verybody's here!" Ruth chirped as the family gathered in the living room. Ever the ringleader, she acted like it was her home instead of Bea's.

Lena Denton was sitting in her usual easy chair with a blank look on her face. Bea couldn't tell from her mother's expression whether she had been the one listening on the telephone line. Max was there, too, apparently cajoled downstairs by his aunts. Bea thought at age fourteen, her son would be easy enough to decipher. But not so. She couldn't tell if Max knew something. The suspense was excruciating.

"So, what brings you ladies in from Sacramento?" Bea asked. She hoped her nervousness wasn't too obvious to the others. She tended to be nervous around her sisters, even during the best of times. "You two rarely visit during the middle of the work week. There must be a special reason you're here today."

Ruth was a high-earning real estate agent, blissfully

busy with clients, showings, and contracts. She could set her own schedule and successfully tended to the needs of her kids as far as Bea could tell, but she never liked to be away for long. Natalie owned a title and escrow company which both benefited from the steady flow of business Ruth referred and provided a reliable foundation for the real estate powerhouse to lean on. To see both Ruth and Natalie away from their bustling, symbiotic businesses like this was unusual.

"Yes, my loves," Lana added, breaking out of her trance. "To what do we owe the pleasure of this visit?"

Bea was relieved to hear her mother speak. Judging by her voice, it didn't seem like Lana was rattled. If she had been listening to the call Bea received, she would most definitely have been rattled. Or so Bea thought.

Ruth and Natalie looked at each other and grinned. They were up to something, that was for sure. Bea was curious, but had a lot on her mind and wanted to get whatever pomp and circumstance the twins had up their sleeves over with as quickly as possible.

"Go on," Bea prompted. "You obviously have something to say. Whatever it is, spit it out."

Max looked down at his hands impatiently and popped a few knuckles. There was probably a video game he'd rather be playing right now. He had only been out of school for a little while and would need to start on his homework soon. Bea thought he looked bothered. She hoped it was because of missing out on a game and not because he had overheard her telephone conversation. Her son was growing up fast. But Bea knew if he had been the one listening in, bringing up such a tense topic would be a chore for Max. He was a quiet introvert who didn't like conflict any more than his mother did. Whatever genes allowed John his ease in the spotlight had not been passed on to his child. When Max spoke up, it was because something was very important to him.

"We have an announcement!" Natalie exclaimed, practically jumping around the room.

"That's right," Ruth confirmed. "We're visiting in the middle of the work week because we are doing work, right here in Rosemary Run."

"Wait," Bea said, raising a hand in anticipation of what she suspected was coming. "What?"

Lana and Max weren't piecing it together yet. Both were clearly confused.

"Are you working from our house today?" Max asked. "You could use my laptop."

Bea shot a loving glance at her sweet boy. He was such a generous soul.

"No, not exactly, but that's a nice offer," Natalie said to her nephew. Bea had always thought Natalie was better with kids than Ruth, even though she hadn't given birth to any of her own. She had a way with them that was plain to see. Max smiled back. He loved his aunts, despite considering them dramatic and crazy.

"Then what?" Max asked.

Natalie and Ruth looked at each other again, reveling in their shared secret. It seemed as though they almost didn't want to tell it, for then it would be out in the open rather than hidden, theirs to share alone.

"Well?" Lana prompted.

"Okay, okay," Ruth said with a smile. "We won't keep

you in suspense any longer. Natalie and I are opening an office for the real estate company and the title company right here in Rosemary Run! And we want Bumble to run it."

Bea was floored. *Was this a cruel trick?*

"Well," Ruth added. "I don't mean Bumble would run it all by herself. We wouldn't expect that. Natalie and I will come into town from time to time to check up on things. And we will be in close touch via phone and email. But Bumble will be Office Manager, if she wants the job."

Bea tried to hide the shock on her face, but wasn't successful. Her twin sisters had picked on her and talked down to her for so many years. The only saving grace was that they didn't live in town and thus didn't have involvement with her day-to-day life. This new arrangement threatened to destroy the carefully constructed sense of peace Bea thought she had carved out for herself. Not to mention, she was insulted at how Ruth and Natalie thought she needed their pity. Bea had a career as an artist, though no one in her family seemed to take it seriously anymore.

"Say thank you, Bea, dear," her mother urged after a moment of tense silence had passed.

"Don't tell her what to say, Grandma," Max interjected. "She can speak for herself."

"It's okay, son," Bea finally said, finding her voice.

Bea thought it was actually a good offer. She might have considered taking it if she weren't faced with being persecuted for her crime. Her art career had, in fact, stalled, even though she hated to admit it.

For a time, before John came into her life and Max

was born, Bea had exhibited in swanky New York City galleries. She had routinely packed posh lofts with wealthy patrons, leaving standing room only. She had often sold out of every piece of artwork she had on hand, then had created new pieces on spec. Those were the days. Life was simpler by comparison.

Bea could not have realized how her world would change when John walked into her gallery. He was in town on a business trip to the Big Apple and just so happened to stumble in. He was older at nearly forty, while Bea was in her mid-twenties. She surprised herself by being interested in an older man. There was something about John that made her feel all grown up and appreciated. He had a charisma which couldn't be denied. And he treated her nicely. Coincidentally, John lived in the wine country town of Rosemary Run, California. The very same Rosemary Run where Bea had grown up and where her parents still lived. It felt like fate. The pair had barely been dating six months when Bea agreed to pack up and move back home to the West Coast to be with her beau. Besides, her father's health was failing, and she wanted to be nearby for what little time he had left.

"Hello? Earth to Bumble Bea," Ruth said, putting a hand on one hip and snapping her little sister back to the present. "We've just made you an offer you would be foolish to refuse. What's the problem?"

Bea noticed how Max bristled at the nickname. Perhaps her son saw family dynamics more clearly than she did.

"Mom already has a job," Max said solidly. "She's a famous artist. She has an art degree and everything."

Bea felt a hand shoot up to cover her mouth. Something about Max's sincere adoration made her suddenly feel like she was falling apart. When it came to her love for her only child, everything else paled by comparison. She didn't care if she sold out art galleries anymore. Not really. She didn't care that her sisters teased her. Or that her marriage had become a mere shell of its former self. She'd gladly trade it all for simple days with Max. Mom duties such as washing his clothes, making her boy dinner, and talking with him about what had happened in school were fulfilling in a way that nothing else had ever been. Bea just wanted more of the same, uninterrupted. After all, in four short years, Max would be off to college and their days of easy togetherness would come to an end. Assuming Bea wasn't taken away sooner to pay for what she'd done. She knew she had to focus all her energy on finding the person who knew about it.

"Nat, Ruthie," Bea began, the nicknames she'd given them not carrying near the same weight as her own. "That's a wonderful, kind offer. It means the world to me. Honestly, I never thought you would extend me such an opportunity. I'm honored."

"She'll do it!" Natalie said, getting ahead of her little sister.

"Not so fast," Max quipped. "She isn't done."

Bea took a deep breath. She knew her sisters would be prone to act badly if she didn't cooperate with their every whim. Bea certainly didn't want to get into the middle of a dramatic scene today, of all days.

"Humph. She's actually going to turn us down," Ruth muttered under her breath. "That little…"

"No need to call names," Lana said quietly. She wanted her daughters to get along, but she had never been able to make it happen. Her husband, Freddy Denton, had been the disciplinarian.

"I'm so sorry," Bea said sheepishly.

4

Thanks to the Denton twins, full-blown chaos had descended on the Hughes household by the time John returned from work. He was home earlier than usual. Bea wondered if someone had urged him to come early. She wondered if the robotic voice had called him and told him about what she'd done. After all, if the caller had her home number, they surely knew how to reach John at the office.

"I see we have company," John grumbled as he came in the back door. The sounds of Ruth and Natalie's loud gabbing took over the space and were impossible to ignore. John gave his wife an obligatory peck on the cheek as she scooted over to greet him.

"We do," Bea whispered, facing John to catch him up privately. "A surprise visit."

John shot her a look of disdain as he set down his briefcase and loosened his tie. "I prefer planning things ahead of time. You know that. I'd say I've been more than accommodating by letting your mother live with us. Isn't that enough? And what are you wearing? You have dried paint all over yourself. Come on, Beatrice, make an effort."

"I know," Bea replied, pleading with her eyes in the hopes he wouldn't make a scene. She couldn't tell him about the phone call which had caused her to spill paint. She couldn't tell him about any of her personal struggles. There was nothing new there.

"Don't mind us, John," Ruth said, boisterously, from across the room. "Natalie and I are heading back to Sacramento shortly. We came to make your wife a generous offer. In true character, she refused."

"How sad," John said, kissing Ruth, and then Natalie, on the cheek. He flashed his best megawatt smile and turned on the charm for their benefit. Bea hated how the three of them treated her like a child. She hated how they talked about her like she wasn't there. "What was the offer?"

"We should probably let her tell you herself," Natalie piped in. "Ruth and I have spent enough energy on our ungrateful little sister today. Suffice to say, we handed her the perfect opportunity to get out of that miserable shed and do something productive with her life. Only heaven knows why she wants to stay in such a rut."

Bea shook her head, but so slightly that no one else noticed. She wasn't sure they would have noticed no matter what she did. A familiar, docile feeling washed over her, pinning her arms at her sides and her mouth shut with its invisible, gooey binding. Bea was used to staying quiet and out of the way. She knew she had lost herself at some point, but her doormat responses had become a habit. A crutch. A punishment even. Maybe she was punishing herself for the bad thing she had done. Either way, it was what everyone expected of her now.

"I'm sorry," Bea said, running her fingers over a section of hard, cracked paint on her blouse.

"Yeah, you said that already," Ruth replied with a snarl. "Your graveling doesn't make it right. You've disrespected your family, Bumble. Have you no shame?"

In the early part of their marriage, John would have come to his wife's defense. He would not have let her sisters talk down to her like this. But things had changed. While other people were watching, John was prone to acting like he was a real peach of a guy and that everything was okay, albeit less than perfect. Behind closed doors though, it was another story. His quick temper and cutting insults were dispensed regularly in Bea's direction.

Bea had tried to leave John once. In fact, she had started up an affair with a good and kind man who lived in a neighboring town by the bay. Travis Earl had been the real thing. The chemistry between them had been off the charts, probably in no small part because he was Bea's age and she thought of him as a peer rather than a father figure. Travis was tall and muscular with a plush head of thick, dark hair which appeared vibrant and oh, so gloriously youthful as compared to John's gray, receding hairline and withering frame. Travis owned his own business building handcrafted furniture and selling it out of a quaint showroom. His back was broad and his hands were strong in a way that John's could never be, given his daily work behind a desk. Travis stirred something deep within Bea. Being with him felt right. Maybe it had something to do with their shared love of creating with their hands. Whatever the case, if circumstances had been different and the incident hadn't happened, Bea could have seen herself splitting up with John, marrying Travis and living happily ever after. It would have been a drastically different existence from the one she was trapped within now.

"Leave her alone," Max said, making his way into the room and hugging his mother's neck. Bea didn't want to lean on him too much. He was still a child. But his attention was her lifeline.

"It's okay, Max," she said to her son. Her voice was strong and calm when she spoke to him. She could hear the difference. A fleeting thought occurred to Bea that her body was like a barometer of sorts. It knew what was right and good. Maybe someday she'd have the courage to listen to it.

"Good evening, sport," John said to his son, walking over to give him a high five. John was usually careful that Max didn't see or hear his ill treatment of Bea. And Bea thanked goodness for that. In Max's young mind, his aunts were the only adversaries Bea needed defending from.

"Hi, Dad," Max replied timidly.

Young Max was irritated with his aunts for picking on Bea. And Bea realized her son was probably frustrated that he had to come to her defense. A part of her knew that she should stand up for herself because it would be better for Max if she did so. The thought of it sent a shiver down her spine. She didn't want to fail her son. Of all the things she didn't want, it was that most of all. But she was just so immobilized with guilt that had turned into shame. She didn't know how she would find her way out.

"Are you hungry, son?" John asked Max.

"Yeah, I am," Max said. He was smack in the middle of that notorious teenage-boy growth phase and he was always hungry.

"Have you prepared anything for dinner?" John asked, turning to his wife and shooting a dirty look in her direction.

Bea's face turned red under the scrutiny of John's words. She had been so caught up by the fear of the anonymous caller and then the drama with her sisters that she hadn't even thought about dinner. She felt like a bad mom. And a bad wife. Yet she wondered how she could expect herself to function normally knowing that her world might crumble at any moment. With another ring of the telephone or a knock on the door, it could all come to an end. The realization was terrifying.

"No, I'm sorry," Bea said, her shoulders slumped forward. "I'll get something together."

"Except that it's too late now," John barked, his intensity surprising her. "We have a house full of people at dinner time and you don't have a single thing prepared." His tone was more aggressive than what he usually displayed around Max. Bea could see her son's face respond. His brow wrinkled and his mouth opened to speak, although he closed it just as quickly while he considered the situation.

As fast as John's stormy mood had been hurtled at Bea, he shifted his attention elsewhere and his sunny charm returned. "Ladies," he said to Bea's sisters. "How about I take everyone out for a nice dinner before you hit the road? You don't want to travel on an empty stomach, do you?"

It was clear to Bea that John enjoyed being the big, important man who could woo everyone with his influence and power. It stoked his ego. The whole thing made her uncomfortable. On this of all evenings, she was revolted by the thought of having to sit through dinner while John ignored her and showered attention on her disrespectful sisters. But he was right. It would be faster and easier to go out for dinner than it would be to prepare a meal for six people.

"Oh, that sounds kind of fabulous," Ruth said, tilting her head to one side and lifting a shoulder up in a flirty pose. "What exactly do you have in mind, John Hughes?"

"I don't know," John said coyly, drawing it out another moment for dramatic effect. "How about we dine at Honey Hog downtown? It's one of my old favorites. They've just reopened after an extensive renovation and I hear it's very well done. Rustic-chic. I've been meaning to take a look, anyway. Food & Wine magazine is set to do a feature article on them next month. It'll be great publicity for the town of Rosemary Run."

"Fancy!" Natalie added. "That sounds wonderful, but are you sure we aren't underdressed for such a distinguished establishment? And you, well, you always see people you know when we're out. We wouldn't want to embarrass you."

John, Ruth, and Natalie turned at once to Bea and gave her a condescending look. Another dig about her clothing and the paint she had spilled on it. John was already wearing a suit, the same as he did every day for work. Ruth and Natalie were both dressed to the nines in the clothing they wore to do business. Even Lana was wearing a skirt and a blouse that would be more than presentable at the high-end restaurant. Max could get by with throwing a sweater over top of his t-shirt and pants. That left Bea, who stood out as obviously underdressed and different. Her family's stares made her feel like another social class altogether. Like she didn't belong with the rest of them. And like she wasn't good enough to be in their presence. *Who did she think she was, anyway?* She knew it without having to be reminded. She was a frumpy middle-aged woman, a failed artist, a substandard mom, and the most unsuccessful, uncouth, and unattractive member of her entire family.

"You ladies look lovely, as usual," John assured the twins. "If my wife can clean herself up to look half as good as you two and your beautiful mother, we'll do just fine."

Bea didn't want to rock the boat or draw any more undue attention to herself, so she got moving. "Give me fifteen minutes," she said.

"Good," Ruth replied. "I'll make sure Mom is ready."

5

Bea glanced at her son as she shuffled up the stairs to make herself presentable for the spur-of-the-moment dinner party. Something about Max was different. He seemed to be tuned in to what she was going through more so than ever before. She wondered if this was just part of growing up and the developmental stage he had reached. At the same time, she couldn't help but wonder if he was seeing her in a new light because of what he had overheard on the phone this afternoon. Her heart skipped a beat as she considered the very real possibility.

When she reached the top of the stairs, Bea paused to take stock of her situation. It was beginning to feel surreal. Her attractive home filled with attractive furniture suddenly felt foreign and hostile. Even though she had picked most of it out and had taken comfort in the beautiful house and furnishings John had provided her, she couldn't help but feel that her residence was actually more like a prison.

Bea moved her hand gently across the wooden banister at the top of the staircase, tracing its lines with her index finger. As she walked down the hallway towards the master bedroom she shared with John, she held her hand up, running her fingertips along the wall and stopping to trace the outline of every framed photo filled with family memories. She looked hard at the faces in each one. For most of the memories featured on her walls, Bea had been pretending. For Max's sake, she had put on a happy face even though she usually felt hollow inside. If Max was seeing the truth of Bea's existence, perhaps it would soon be time to reconsider her strategy.

"Beatrice," John called up the stairs in a booming voice. "Don't doddle. Everyone is waiting on you."

Bea shook her head and rolled her eyes, but didn't respond. She hated the way his voice sounded. She hated the way he called her Beatrice. Only her dad had called her that.

Freddy Denton had been a good father to Bea. He was warm, smart as a whip, and encouraging to all three of his daughters. Everyone else seemed to have treated the twins differently. Maybe it was the novelty of their pairing. They weren't identical twins, but they were both stunningly beautiful, even as young children. Adults lavished them with praise and were mesmerized by the two of them, resulting in Bea being nothing more than an afterthought. But not Freddy. He saw Beatrice. Really saw her. His love and support were the best things in Bea's life. They were why she knew how to love Max unconditionally. Lana was nice enough and had been a good mother, but Bea owed the best parts of herself to her dad. She hadn't been ready to lose him when she did.

It was a result of Freddy's insistence that Bea went to New York City to pursue her dream. If she'd had any idea that his health would decline while she was away, she never would have left.

Sometimes, Bea wondered if her dad knew he was sick when he sent her off. He would have wanted only the best for her, so she could imagine him having done something like that. It still hurt her to think about. Freddy wanted the world to be her oyster. He wanted his youngest daughter to have and be everything she wanted. His dedication to her happiness was absolute. But Bea would have rather spent his final years near her dad. She would have taken care of him and done anything he needed. No task would have been too tedious and no time spent a waste. Nothing lasting had come out of Bea's so-called art career anyway.

Bea wondered what her dad would think if he could see her now. She also wondered how things could have gone so terribly wrong in her life. Was it inevitable? Was it the twins' birth right to outshine their younger sister?

It was not lost on Bea how John had come into her life right around the same time as her dad left it. If she was honest with herself, she knew she had been looking to fill the void the loss Freddy's passing had created. That was no way to begin a marriage. It was certainly no way to sustain a marriage either, which was why Travis came into the picture.

Sometimes, when Bea needed to escape her circumstances, she'd close her eyes and imagine herself living in this big, beautiful house with Travis rather than with John. As she walked into the master bedroom and closed the door behind her, she squinted her eyes until she could see Travis on the bed, waiting to embrace her. She and John scarcely made love, if you could even call it that. It was more a necessary physical release. But it didn't happen often, and it always felt forced to Bea. She longed for Travis' loving touch and attentive sexual healing. The feel of his skin against her own set her entire body alight. It was unlike anything she had ever experienced before. Or since.

"Beatrice," John called again from downstairs, more forcefully this time and so loud Bea could hear it through the closed bedroom door. "What are you doing up there? Hurry!"

Obliging, Bea stepped into her closet and pulled out a dress, all while keeping her eyes narrowed and Travis on her mind. It was a blue dress, featuring a floral print and a plunging neckline that fell just off Bea's shoulders. A feminine ruffle danced along the bottom edge and promised to sway with her every move. It might have been too sexy for this evening's family dinner. It might have been too sexy for old John Hughes under any circumstances. But she decided to wear it, anyway. A black shrug would cover her shoulders and tone the outfit down, but in Bea's mind, she would pretend she was sneaking off to meet Travis. She would cooperate with John while mentally being somewhere else entirely. The fantasy would help her get through the evening. It would take her mind off of not only John and her nasty twin sisters, but it would help Bea push back the terror that came every time her thoughts wandered to this afternoon's telephone call.

As Bea held the dress against herself and sized the choice up in her full-length mirror, she imagined Travis looking at her with delight and ravaging her with his eyes. She imagined him stepping close and breathing in her scent as he placed his thick, warm lips on her neck and his strong hands around her waist. Travis wanted her in a hungry, primal way that John never had. And Bea wanted Travis, too. In fact, she wanted nothing more than to be with him. It had taken every ounce of strength she had to push him away.

As Bea slid into the dress, then plopped down at her dressing table to freshen her makeup and put on some earrings, the doorbell rang. The Hughes' home sat on a three acre lot and the closest neighbor was a fair distance away. The doorbell didn't ring often, though it certainly got more use than the landline telephone. Bea froze when she heard its chime as a wave of panic moved through her body. She stood up, forcing her legs to carry her to the bedroom window. Her movements were jerky, those of a threatened animal.

The roofline of the front porch prevented Bea from seeing who was standing at the front door. But she didn't need to. The rain had stopped and she could see the yard out front clearly. There, in her own driveway, was a police car. The words Rosemary Run Police Department were emblazoned on each side, blue and red lights flashing.

At a dizzying speed, Bea's body turned itself inside out. She didn't even make it to the bathroom before she leaned over and retched, splattering hot vomit on her pretty party dress.

6

B ea wiped her mouth haphazardly and then raced out of the bedroom to crouch at the top of the stairs. She had to hear what was happening.

"Mayor Hughes," a masculine voice said from the front entrance. "Sorry to disturb you at home, sir."

It was Officer James Tatum. Bea had attended school with him. She recognized his voice right away.

Oh, God, he's here to arrest me.

"No need to apologize, James," John said in his easy-going mayor persona. "What can I do for you this evening?"

"What's happening?" Ruth chirped as she followed John to the door.

"Is something wrong, Officer?" Natalie echoed.

There was a pause. It felt to Bea like an eternity. She wondered where Max was and if he was scared. She had pictured this day a million times. She hadn't expected to be wearing a party dress when it happened.

Finally, James spoke again. "Sir, how about we step

outside so we can talk privately? I don't want to disturb your guests."

"We're his family," Natalie clarified. "Well, Bumble Bea's family, anyway. Don't you remember us from school? We were a couple of years ahead of you. But younger than your sister."

"Cate, right?" Ruth asked.

"Oh, yeah," James replied, remembering. "You're the Denton twins. Good to see you again."

"The pleasure is ours," Natalie said, winking.

"Stop it, Natalie," Ruth insisted. "He's married, you know. I've seen him and his pretty wife around town."

"That's right," James said. "Rebecca. My wife's name is Rebecca. And thank you. I think she's pretty, too, but I may be biased."

"Ah, I see," Natalie said, sounding disappointed.

"I thought you two moved out of town," James said. "Was it San Francisco?"

"Sacramento," Ruth clarified. "But we're opening a new office here in Rosemary Run. It will be a joint venture between my real estate firm and my sister's title and escrow company. Keep us in mind if you're ever in the market for a new home."

"I'll do that," James replied politely. "Congratulations to you both."

Bea could hear John breathing deeply. He was trying to stay calm for his audience, but he was growing frustrated.

"Officer Tatum," John said when there was a break in the conversation. "I'm happy to step outside as you suggested. Let's do that."

Bea could hear the front door swing open wider and then close hard. She shook as she shifted into a fetal position. She hoped no one came up the stairs and saw her like this. Most of all, she hoped she would have time to explain things to Max and her mother before she was arrested.

Did they allow murderers time to explain things to their loved ones?

There. She had thought it. She was a murderer.

Now what?

7

Somehow, Bea found the strength to get back to the bedroom and clean herself up. She didn't want to be stuck wearing a dress in jail. Or prison. Or wherever it was they would take her. She washed her face, brushed her teeth, and put on a sensible pair of jeans. She chose to layer with a sweatshirt over a long-sleeved shirt, both over top of a t-shirt. She wanted to be prepared for any temperature. She put on warm socks and a pair of comfortable running shoes.

As Bea dressed herself, she thought about how she was trying to exercise some element of control over her life. It was human nature. If she couldn't handle the important matters she faced and was about to lose her very freedom, then by God, she could choose the clothing she wore.

When Bea had envisioned this day, she hadn't imagined that her old classmate James Tatum would be the arresting officer. He was a good guy who would be disappointed to know about her wrongdoing. He was the kind of guy you wanted to believe in you. The kind who inspired you to be better. What a mess.

Bea had been careful not to search the web for anything related to her misdeeds or potential imprisonment. She knew the police would seize her electronic devices as part of their investigation once she was apprehended. She didn't want any incriminating evidence which could look worse and lengthen her sentence. As a result, much of what she knew about women in prison she had learned from television shows like *Orange is the New Black*. It wasn't much, but it was something.

She hadn't contacted an attorney. She didn't want to look guilty.

Bea intended to do her time and get back to her son as soon as humanly possible. She just hoped that she had been around long enough to see him through his formative years. She hoped he could move forward without her now, at age fourteen. And beyond that, she hoped to be released in time to meet her grandchildren away from the prying eyes of prison guards.

Bea hadn't told another soul, but she had prepared for this day. In a brown box in the attic under art supplies which had been carefully placed as a decoy, Bea kept a cache of items meant to help Max get through the time she was away. She had birthday cards made out for each of the next thirty years. She realized thirty may have been overkill, but she wanted there to be enough. She had also written letters for Max to open on several special days including his first date, his first car and drivers license, his high school graduation, his first day of college, his college graduation, the first day of his first real job after college, his engagement, his wedding, and the day he becomes a father. The letters were gut-wrenching to write. Many mornings while Max was in school, Bea had composed the letters and then sealed them neatly with instructions written across the front. John had never noticed the time she'd spent. He had simply assumed she had been painting in her studio.

But that wasn't all. Bea had made videos in which she talked to Max about situations he might have to face as part of growing up. In one video, Bea presented tips for choosing the right college environment. In another, she provided guidance about what to do when her son suffers his inevitable first break-up with a girlfriend. She could envision Max on each of those special days, his face stained with tears because his mom wasn't there. The whole situation was horrible, top to bottom and beginning to end.

As she made the videos and wrote the letters, Bea had felt like a terminally ill patient preparing for her own death. She supposed it was a death of sorts. It was a death of life as they'd known it. It was most likely the death of John's political career. It was the death of Max's childhood along with any illusion that life was simple and fair. And it was the death of Bea's personal hopes and dreams. Although if she was being honest with herself, Bea knew that particular death had occurred a long time ago.

She had gone over it in her mind countless times. On the day she was arrested-- *today*-- she would tell her mother and her best friend Gabrielle Radnor about the box. She'd give them explicit guidance on how to secure the contents somewhere off the property so that John wouldn't be able to interfere. Then, she'd ask them to distribute the contents to Max as the important days came. It was all Bea knew to do in her absence. She had done the best she could for her dear, sweet boy, given the circumstances.

"Beatrice," John called from downstairs. She hadn't heard him come back in. *This is it. It's time.* "Will you come down here, please?"

Bea closed her eyes and took a big, long breath in. One of her last as a free woman. She set her smartphone down on her nightstand, since she wouldn't be needing it where she was going. Then, she raised her head high and walked out of the bedroom to face her fate. She felt proud of her own courage. As bad as this situation was, Bea felt relieved that it would finally be out in the open. Hiding the truth had taken a toll on her.

"Coming," Bea replied to her husband, her voice stronger than it had been in a long time. She climbed down the stairs, one by one, her bravery becoming fortified with every step. When she reached the bottom, she walked through the kitchen and into the living room, ready to meet Officer James Tatum at the front entrance. Only the door was closed. He wasn't there.

8

"Are you serious, Bumble?" Ruth quipped. "*This* is your idea of dressing nice to dine at Honey Hog?"

"Come on, Beatrice," John said under his breath. "Are you trying to embarrass yourself?"

Bea was confused. *Where was Officer Tatum? Why was everyone pretending like nothing was wrong?* She cleared her throat. "Who… Um, I heard someone at the door."

"It was a work thing. For Dad," Max explained.

"Officer Tatum had some business with John," Lana added. She could see her daughter's distress and wanted to help. "You remember James Tatum, don't you, Bea? He was in your class in school."

Bea's mind reeled. She struggled to make sense of what was happening. She had been so sure that she was about to be arrested. "Yeah," she replied to her mom. "I remember him. What kind of business was he here to discuss?" She wanted to know more. *Needed* to know more.

"Nothing for you to be concerned about," John said.

"But I'd like to know who was at the door of my house," Bea said, persisting. "Our house..."

"I guess it isn't every day that a police officer knocks on your door," Lana added with a smile. John was stuck, having to play the role of a good guy since others were watching. Bea was grateful to her mother for chiming in and forcing John to act civil. Lana probably understood more about the dynamics between Bea and John than she let on. She had been there to observe them every single day for a while now. No matter how well John hid it, there were surely signs that things were less than rosy in their marriage.

"No big deal," John reiterated. "James was here to talk to me about a sensitive matter which he felt necessitated an in-person discussion rather than a phone call." John looked at Bea as he emphasized the words *phone call* and her heart skipped another few beats. Although maybe it was her imagination and John had emphasized nothing at all. The back-and-forth was exhausting. Bea was half tempted to confess and turn herself in just to get it over with. But she would never do such a thing as long as Max was around. She couldn't. He still needed her.

"Why don't you get changed for dinner, dear?" Lana asked Bea. "Everything is okay down here."

"Okay, Mom," Bea said, swallowing hard. "I just... I'm sorry, everyone. I mean... I'll be right back." Ruth and Natalie snickered, but kept their comments to themselves.

Gathering her composure, Bea walked back up the stairs, feeling both grateful for her freedom and a little disappointed that she'd have to remain hypervigilant going forward. It was positively exhausting. She retrieved her phone from the nightstand and then went into her closet again, this time selecting a simple mauve pencil skirt and pink blouse to wear. She didn't have the desire to try the sexy, off-the-shoulder number a second time. Her mood was deflated. She wasn't sure that even Travis Earl himself could lift her spirits, had he been there in the flesh.

When she was dressed, Bea went back downstairs, prepared to play the part of the diminutive, obedient wife. "I'm ready," she announced. "Shall we all ride together?" John owned a large SUV which would easily hold all six of them. Bea knew her husband liked to drive, especially when he was entertaining.

"Sure thing," Natalie said. "The restaurant isn't far."

"John," Ruth began. "If you don't mind driving, I think it would be nice for us to go together as one big, happy family."

Max smiled. Like all kids, he was a sucker for everyone being together. Bea understood. It was a good wish. She would have liked the same thing if it could have somehow been real and based on mutual respect.

"It would be my pleasure," John replied as he gestured towards the back door.

Following his lead, the group made their way outside like old times. This particular group didn't get together all that often anymore. But there had been a period back when Max was a baby when they'd had frequent dinner dates. It wasn't long after Freddy died, and the rest of the family had made a concerted effort to spend time together. Bea felt a pang of sadness as she thought about how things used to be so much better. Even between her and her sisters. She wondered if they could ever get that back again.

But Max's mood was cheerful and Bea liked to see her son feeling good. He paused to squat and scratch Marmalade under the chin as they walked past. *That's what this is about,* Bea thought to herself. *Another day of his happiness.* She smiled along with him as they climbed into the SUV and started down the long, meandering driveway.

As they approached the mailbox at the end of the drive and John began to turn onto the main road, a woman in a little black station wagon pulled out in front and stopped them.

"What now?" John asked thinly, trying to hide his irritation.

"That's Mrs. White," Max said cheerfully from the back seat. "You know her, Dad. She lives next door."

"Ah, yes, I do," John replied. "But what is she doing here?"

Myra White was a nosy neighbor with far too much time on her hands. Had her house been closer, she would have probably been peering in the Hughes family's windows on a daily basis. As it was, she had to do her snooping from a bit of a distance.

Myra's husband had divorced her and left a sizable alimony benefit after a cliché fling with his secretary became widely known around town. It had happened a few years ago. Their kids were both in college now and Myra was an empty nester who had spent the past two decades as a homemaker. Not knowing what else to do with herself and stabilized by her ex-husband's financial support, Myra had hulled up inside her house. Bea wondered what she did in there all day.

"She probably saw the police car," Lana offered. Lana had spent more time with Myra than anyone else in the Denton-Hughes household. She sometimes invited her over for afternoon tea and a game of cards.

"I see," John confirmed. "I'll handle this," he said, putting the vehicle in park and stepping outside.

Bea noticed herself beginning to perspire. Every interaction seemed to send her into a tailspin today. Danger was around every corner. "She looks upset," Bea remarked as she watched Myra get out of her car and approach John.

"The drama!" Ruth exclaimed. "It's like a regular episode of *Cops* around here." Lana shot Ruth a look that said to leave it alone.

Bea's mom was a sweet old lady who didn't get into the middle of conflicts if she could help it. Her laid-back personality meant that she was taken more seriously when she expressed a firm opinion. All three of her girls respected their mother.

They sat in the car, watching carefully to see what would transpire between Myra and John, who now stood less than a foot apart from one another. They spoke in what appeared to be hushed tones. The conversation must have been intense because Myra began waving her arms around as she talked. She was doing most of the talking and John was listening. Bea's heart sank further into her chest the longer she watched. She just knew they were talking about her. If the anonymous caller could find her phone number, they could easily find her neighbor's number.

"What a day," Bea mused, attempting to test her voice. It was squeaky and unsure. She could hear it. The others turned to look at her, but didn't say a word.

"What do you think they're talking about?" Max asked innocently. "I'm trying to read their lips, but they keep turning so I can't get a clear view." He was curious, the way any teenager would be. Bea thought it funny how Max wouldn't pay much attention when an adult was trying to tell him something directly, yet he was mesmerized to the point of trying to read lips when a conversation happened that he wasn't supposed to be a part of.

"I don't know," Natalie said. "But Ruth is right; it's all very dramatic. If this isn't an episode of *Cops*, it could be one of those shows about housewives."

"Oh, even better," Ruth added with a chuckle. "*Real Housewives of Rosemary Run*. That has a nice ring to it." Again, Lana turned and gave the girls a look that told them to let it rest. They did. For the time being.

Bea's mind continued to spin as she worked herself into a near anxiety attack, then talked herself down only to begin the cycle again. She couldn't take it anymore. She had to move. In a burst, she opened the door beside her and got out of the SUV.

"Where are you going?" Lana asked.

"To see what they're talking about," Bea replied.

"I'm not so sure that's a good idea," Lana said.

Something was different about Lana this afternoon, the same as there was something different about Max. Bea didn't know what to think about who had been listening in on the telephone line, but she couldn't have guessed if her life depended on it. It might have been Max. Or it might have been her mother. It also might have been Ruth or Natalie since they were apparently having tea with Lana when the call came in. Not to mention, John might have been contacted. Or James might have been contacted. So it wouldn't be a stretch to think that Myra might have been contacted. Bea felt like everyone around her knew. And she had no idea what to do about it.

"Myra, hello," Bea said as she walked towards her husband and neighbor, ignoring her mother's warnings. "I haven't seen you in a while. How have you been?"

"Beatrice, go back to the car," John said. "I've got this under control."

"Nonsense," Bea said to her husband, turning on a little charm of her own. "It looks like Myra has something to discuss. She looks quite concerned. What kind of neighbor would I be if I didn't hop out to listen and offer my support?"

Myra seemed to like Bea's answer. She was a jaded divorcee who almost certainly had ill will towards men at this point. Bea thought perhaps she could use this to her advantage.

"Hello there, Bea," Myra said sweetly. "Lovely to see you, too. But it's nothing to be bothered about, just like your husband said." Myra shot a knowing glance at John as if they were in on something together.

John shifted his weight back on his heels and put both hands in his pockets. "Fine. I'll fill you in. After this afternoon's rain, there was more water than usual running from our yard into Myra's," John explained. "She was letting me know so we could check our drainage situation in case we need to get a landscaper out to make some modifications."

"That's right," Myra said, unconvincingly. "Now that I've mentioned it, I'll run along and leave you to your outing. Sorry to disturb!" Then she got back into her station wagon and drove away so fast there wasn't even time to buckle her seatbelt.

Bea wrinkled her brow. She knew they were lying. No one talked about extra rainwater as intensely as she'd seen Myra and John talking. Besides, Myra was a busybody who usually would have taken time to ask prying questions as she chatted with every last person in the SUV. Something else was going on.

Did they know?

"You had better remember your place," John said coldly to his wife. He wore a smile on his face so the passengers in the car wouldn't be able to tell how icy his words were, but Bea felt it, sure as a winter's frost. She hated being scolded like a child, right in her own yard. "Mind your business," John continued. "You don't belong in my discussions. You had better hear and believe me. Or else."

Bea looked down, losing the momentum she had gathered before she got out of the vehicle. What had she been thinking? John would not let her be privy to any serious discussion. She would have to figure out some other way to learn exactly what he knew.

9

Honey Hog was every bit as swanky and gorgeous as Bea had imagined. Exposed wooden beams lined the arched ceiling while elegant pendant lights dangled down towards the reclaimed wood tables set with white cloth napkins, artisan dinnerware, and crystal vases filled with sprigs of fresh-cut rosemary. The new owners had invested a pretty penny to renovate the place from top to bottom. John was right. The revamped restaurant would make a good name for Rosemary Run as news of its re-opening spread far and wide.

Bea ordered pork brisket for herself and deviled eggs, cheddar biscuits, and gourmet coleslaw to be shared with the table. To wash it all down, the adults enjoyed homegrown Rosemary Run red wine, as was customary. When you live in wine country, you might as well partake in the fruits produced by the region. Every morsel of food and every drop of wine tasted heavenly. At first, Bea hadn't been sure she'd be able to eat. But once she smelled the food and took a couple of bites, she realized how hungry she was. She hadn't eaten since breakfast and was famished. The tremendous stress she'd been under had probably taken a lot out of her body.

Bea tried her best to relax and enjoy the evening, given the fact that just a few hours prior she had thought she'd be spending it in custody. As she looked at her son and her mother, she was grateful to be with them now. Luckily, Max, Lana, and Bea were at one end of the table while John, Ruth, and Natalie were at the other. Bea was stuck sitting by her husband because it would have looked odd if she hadn't been at his side. But the positioning afforded her the luxury of turning her attention toward her mother and son for much of the evening.

The three of them talked about what Max was working on in class and how it compared to when Bea had been his age and a student at the same high school. Lana remembered. She told Max a few fun stories about Bea's adventures in high school marching band. They laughed together about how Bea could never seem to get her buttons polished brightly enough for uniform inspection, and how she was disappointed to learn that her parents could barely hear her flute in the stands when the band performed from the field. Max had opted out of marching band, but was signed up for the debate team and men's soccer. It was only a few weeks into the school year, but many of the kids Max was in class with had been together since they were little ones in grade school. He was having a good experience so far and Bea was glad.

"Say, sport," John offered to his son, trying to get in on the conversation. "How are those grades coming along? You know, now that you're in high school those grades matter more than they used to. Your GPA will determine what kind of college you get into." Bea resented John's prodding. She didn't believe in putting pressure on kids about grades. And besides, Max wouldn't be applying to college for a full three years. Did he really have to concern himself with that right now?

"I know, Dad," Max said shyly. "You've told me a lot of times."

"I know I have," John replied. "I want to be sure it's at the forefront of your mind. Maybe if you do really well, you can go to my alma mater-- Sanford."

"Easy," Bea said, in a rare warning to her husband. "Let him be a kid awhile longer."

Natalie and Ruth looked nervous to see Bea asserting herself. If Bea didn't know better, she would have thought there was a concerted effort to keep her beaten down. Meanwhile, John glanced at a table on the far side of the restaurant filled with men in business suits. He was grandstanding, hoping they would hear him. *Always campaigning*, Bea thought. *How repulsive.*

"I might, Dad," Max answered. "I don't know what I want to study yet. Maybe I'll go to art school, like Mom." Bea sat up straight and smiled upon hearing this.

That's my boy.

"Don't be silly," John said as he spit out a sip of his wine. "There's no future in art school. Just look at your mother." The wine was causing John to let down his guard. As Bea came to think of it, Max wasn't usually around when John drank. She hoped John wouldn't say anything that would be too upsetting for their son to hear. But then again, maybe Max could get an even better idea of what his father was really like. It might ultimately be a good thing.

"Mom paints very beautiful pictures," Max said, sounding defensive. "I like her pictures. Her paintings."

"I know you do, sport," John said quietly, tousling the top of his son's hair and seeming to reel himself back in. At least a little. He raised his glass and took another big gulp of wine then, he again glanced at the table of businessmen in suits across the room. He raised his voice louder and began to speak once more. "But Max, son, I believe you could have a promising career in politics if we get you the proper education. You could be a chip off the old block."

Lana began to speak but then covered her mouth with one hand, thinking better of it. Bea wished her mother would speak up. Max should hear from multiple loved ones on this topic to avoid being forced down a path that isn't of his own choosing.

Bea's blood was boiling now. Her anger towards John was taking her mind off of her other worries. This small comfort made her delve full force into her feelings of rage. "John," she said sternly. "Max is entitled to make his own decisions about what to study in college when it's time. I, for one, will support him no matter what he decides."

"What a joke," John said in his most condescending tone. Even Ruth and Natalie looked surprised. Maybe the two of them hadn't realized just how disrespectful John could be. "Your mother doesn't have a career," he continued. "Not a real one that earns money, anyway. Do you want to end up like her? If I weren't around to take care of her, she'd have to... Well, I don't know. I suppose she'd have to become a waitress at a restaurant like this one." It was a calculated insult. Bea had worked as a waitress in high school at this very restaurant, though it was under different management and called Western Steakhouse back then.

"Wow," Natalie said. "That was a lot."

"You do know Bumble worked at this restaurant back when it was Western Steakhouse, don't you, John?" Ruth asked.

Bea thought it odd how the twins always seemed to speak in sets. One rarely said anything without the other echoing some obligatory add-on comment. But she didn't mind right now. She was grateful to see them feeling protective of her for a change.

"My point exactly," John said.

"John," Lana began, calmly but surely. "Freddy and I were always proud of each of our daughters, Bea included. You're right, she worked hard as a waitress during high school to save up extra money to put gas in her car. We weren't wealthy, but we did okay. We were able to support Bea through art school. We were happy to do so because that was her chosen field. I hope Max will be given the same opportunity to make his own decisions."

Max turned to his grandma and gave her a big, approving smile as he nodded his head. It was more than Lana had ever said to John before in her daughter or grandson's defense and the timing could not have been better as far as Bea was concerned. Normally, Bea would have avoided making a dramatic scene at all costs. But tonight she felt like a tea kettle full of steam and ready to blow. Besides, John was the one creating the tension. Not her.

John scoffed. "That might be true, Lana. But a lot of good it did. Your daughter is nothing but a drain on my wealth, generosity, and patience. If you knew some of the things I've had to do for her, you'd be singing a different tune."

Now it was Bea's turn to scoff. "And if I tallied up the things I've had to do for you," she said to John. "We'd be here all evening. For starters, I've washed your clothes. I've cooked your food. I've cleaned your house. I've dressed up and smiled politely for the endless stream of people you've been desperate to impress. Not to mention, I've raised your son. And for all of it, you've been ungrateful. I've become a shell of my former self thanks to your insults and mistreatment. And for what? Aside from my dear Max, who is the best thing to ever happen in my life, none of it has been worth it."

Everyone at the table was uncomfortable now. Other guests in the restaurant were taking notice. The men in business suits who John had been so preoccupied with were looking in his direction.

"Yeah, is that so?" John asked, turning in his chair and placing one arm on the table and the other around the back of his wife's. It was a territorial pose. He thought he owned her. All bought and paid for.

"Yes, it is," Bea replied.

"Fine," John said, leaning closer. "Then I'll stop protecting your secrets." Bea froze like a deer in headlights.

What secrets? Should she call his bluff? Or was he serious?

"Fine," she returned. "Then I'll stop playing nice in the interest of your political career. God knows nearly every decision we've made during our marriage has been for that reason alone. I'm sick and tired of it. You're nothing but a bitter old man who wants to appear more powerful than he really is. I see through your charade, Mayor John Hughes."

Bea stood up, gathered her things, and moved to the back of Max's chair. "Come on, Max," she said. "Let's take a walk."

Lana, Natalie, and Ruth looked around nervously, hoping to avoid a strained ride home alone with John. Bea was sure that the ladies in her life now wished they had driven separately. This was no happy family.

"A walk to where?" John asked, incredulous.

Bea ignored him. "I'm serious, Max," she said. "Come with me. Right now."

"Where are we going?" Max asked, getting up. Bea knew her son was asking more than simply where they were going in the next few minutes. She knew things with John had reached a boiling point and that they'd never be the same. Max was asking where they were going *in life*. He was asking what would happen to them and if everything would be okay. Bea gave Max her most reassuring look, but she honestly didn't know what to tell him.

"Go, son," John growled. "Go be a mama's boy. That's the truth of what you are, anyway. You won't get far. You'll come crawling back. Both of you."

Max looked stunned at his father's words. And Bea's heart broke for him. She hadn't expected this. Not exactly. The relief felt satisfying, but not at Max's expense.

As Bea and Max turned and began to excuse themselves from the dinner table, they heard a boom so loud that it sounded like a bolt of lightning had struck nearby. People in the restaurant screamed and several stood up and ran out the front door. A little girl seated nearby began to cry big, pitiful tears. Bea didn't have to turn back to see what had made the noise. She already knew.

John's roar came next. He stood up, kicking pieces of the now broken table in front of him as he bellowed like an angry grizzly. He was in a full-on rage, seeing red. There was no stopping him now. He began bucking around and thrashing, destroying chairs and dinnerware as he went. People who hadn't already left the building pulled smartphones out of their pockets and handbags to record their mayor's meltdown. Within minutes, it would be all over the Internet and all over the news.

Bea turned to her mother and sisters, putting one arm around Lana and the other securely around Max. "Let's go," she said. "We're leaving together."

"Bea," Natalie said to her little sister in the most sincere voice as she placed a hand gently on her arm. "We had no idea. I'm so sorry."

10

B ea's palms were sweaty as she picked up the receiver to one of the few public telephones left in town. She inserted a couple of coins into the slot and dialed the number she knew by heart. He picked up after the first ring.

"Hello?"

"Someone knows. Well, more than one person, probably. We need to talk right away. When can we meet?"

"Oh," he said simply. "And after all these years." Bea didn't reply. It was all she could do to steady her breathing. "Tomorrow morning. Ten a.m. at my building. Use the back door and I'll buzz you in."

11

Bea didn't go home that night. At least, not for long. With her mother and sisters, she and Max hired a rideshare service. The driver took them to the house and waited outside while they packed a few things.

Natalie and Ruth were treating Bea better than they had in years. They both offered their homes up for those who had been displaced from the Hughes house. Lana agreed to stay with Natalie for a while, which was good. Natalie lived alone and had two guest rooms available. Truth be told, Lana probably should have been staying with Natalie all along. She was the only one of the three sisters who didn't yet have a family of her own. The logistics made sense. The pair of them agreed to keep Marmalade for a while as well. Bea didn't want any living creature left under John's roof and subjected to his rage.

Bea considered taking Natalie's other guest room for herself and Max, but Sacramento was too far to commute to school and she didn't want her son missing out. Next, she thought about staying at her friend Gabrielle's. It was late and Gabby had no idea what was going on, but she didn't need to. She was the kind of friend who would be there for Bea with no questions asked. The arrangement felt like an imposition, though, because Gabby's boyfriend Miles had recently moved into her loft. Bea didn't want to dampen the couple's early days of living together with her very real problems. Finally, Bea settled on a generous offer from her twin sisters and let them put her and Max up in a hotel room. It was just for a few weeks until Bea got things sorted. Now that they understood what she had been subjected to, the twins felt sympathetic towards Bea's situation and had stopped teasing her. Normally, Bea would have rather starved than accepted their assistance. But they seemed to genuinely want to help and Bea needed the hand.

"I told you they were nice underneath all of their prickliness," Max said to his mom about his aunts as the two of them used the cash Ruth and Natalie had given them to check into the hotel. "I knew it. They love us."

"You were right," Bea confirmed. "My sisters really came through in a big way tonight. I'm surprised, but grateful." Bea scanned the lobby of the hotel for familiar faces as the clerk entered her information into his computer. She didn't want John to know where they were staying. At least, not yet.

"What are you looking around for, Mom?" Max asked. "Or, who?" There was so much for Bea to explain to her boy. Too much. It would take time and deliberate planning if she were to make it all make sense.

"No one in particular," she lied. It hurt her as it came

out of her mouth. She didn't want to lie to her son. "You know what, that's not true," Bea quickly clarified.

"Okay," Max said, confused.

Bea leaned down to talk to her son without the desk clerk overhearing. "The truth is, I don't want your father to know where we are. I'm not sure what condition he's in tonight and I think it's best if we keep some distance." Max nodded, but didn't say a word. "You understand, right?"

"Yeah, I do," he said. Bea thought his voice sounded suddenly too grown-up. She hated what John had done to them.

As Max slept that night, Bea laid in the bed on the other side of the room wide awake. She stared at the ceiling and went over things again and again in her mind. Within the span of a single day, she had gone from a relatively predictable existence to a future that was uncertain. But for some reason, it felt like progress. She willed herself to close her eyes and lie perfectly still until finally, she drifted off to sleep.

12

Bright and early the next morning, Bea put on a v-neck, floral-print blouse and a pair of flattering jeans, then walked Max to school. The hotel's proximity to his high school made for a comfortable stroll through downtown. John's office was less than a block in the other direction, but Bea doubted he was there. After last night's tantrum, she wasn't sure he'd be there ever again except to collect his things. *Did they let mayors who destroyed restaurants in a blind rage remain in office?* Surely not. For all she knew, he had been arrested last night and had spent the night in jail. She had purposely avoided news and social media for the past twelve hours.

Once Bea saw Max off and knew he was safely in the building, she turned her attention towards the next task at hand. It was time to get herself a car. The one she had been driving for the past few years was in John's name. She didn't want to rely on anything that could be taken from her on a whim or at a moment's notice. She kicked herself for not getting things in her own name sooner.

Here she was, a thirty-something adult moving through the world like a child. John's child. Bea scarcely had more independence than Max did. It was time for that to change.

She began with a rental car since it would take a while to work out a permanent solution. With more of the cash in hand that Natalie and Ruth had given her, Bea walked back past the hotel and a few more blocks towards the outskirts of downtown until she reached a rental car lot. There, she paid cash to rent a sensible silver sedan for the next week. *Thank God I kept my driver's license*, Bea thought to herself. There had been a point a few months ago when John had almost talked her out of renewing it. Looking back, she now realized that was insane. She wasn't certain what she had been thinking. But she was beginning to think clearly again, like she used to before she became filled with self-doubt and low self-esteem at the hands of John's cruelty.

The next order of business made Bea's heart race for good and bad reasons all at the same time. She would pay a visit to the person who had been with her and Max the night the incident happened a decade ago. She had to warn him. It was only fair. He deserved to know what she did so he could make his own decisions about how to respond.

Bea climbed into her new rental car and put her sunglasses on, feeling the cool September air against her skin. Then she sped out of town and towards the bay.

13

"Bea, babe, look at you. You are as drop-dead gorgeous as ever," Travis said as he opened the door and laid eyes on her. "What has it been? Nine years now? Ten? You don't age."

Bea felt her cheeks become warm, flush with the blood that was suddenly pumping strong throughout her body and making her feel alive in all the best ways. She loved it when Travis called her babe.

"Hello to you, too," she said coyly. She couldn't have hidden her smile if she'd had to.

"I wish the circumstances were better," Travis mused. "But I have to say, I'm awfully glad to see you."

"The feeling is mutual."

They stood sizing each other up for a minute without saying anything more. The chemistry between the two of them was palpable. Bea thought about how she genuinely liked the man standing in front of her. If only things had been different.

"Well, come on in," Travis finally said. "I don't

suppose I should leave you standing out there on the landing all day." Bea nodded politely and followed him inside. She had been to his place plenty of times when they were seeing each other, but that was a long time ago.

Travis' apartment was a charming loft with high ceilings and exposed brick situated above his furniture store. The structure was built in the 1920s without an interior staircase, but Travis didn't mind. He quite liked having to climb the exterior stairs to enter his living quarters. Something about the setup was rough and tumble, just like him. His place looked exactly the same as Bea remembered it.

"Everything is just the same," she commented as she looked around the loft.

"That's right," Travis said with a chuckle. "You caught me. Here I am, frozen in time. Waiting on you to come back and be with me." Bea blushed. She wasn't sure he was kidding. "But," Travis added. "I don't mean to make you uncomfortable."

"Oh, no," Bea said, absentmindedly twirling the silver wedding ring around on her finger. "Don't worry about it."

Travis noticed her gesture. "Mayor's wife, huh? That must be a pretty good gig, if you can get it."

"Something like that," Bea said. "But looks can be deceiving." She hadn't yet decided how much she wanted to tell Travis about her marriage to John. He'd known before that their relationship was a cold and loveless one. He could assume that nothing much had changed.

"I hope John Hughes is good to you, at least," Travis

said, tilting his head and lowering one eyebrow. "Because if he isn't…"

"I'm fine," Bea said, diverting attention away from her husband. She wasn't ready to discuss him.

"Are you sure?" Travis asked. "Because your face doesn't look fine when I mention John's name."

"I'm alright," she insisted. "Truly. It's a story for another time."

"Then I look forward to hearing it," Travis said as he reached one big, strong hand up and placed it on Bea's shoulder. His touch electrified her body and threatened to make her melt like putty.

Nervous and unsure of exactly what to do with herself, Bea volleyed the attention back in Travis' direction. "How about you?" she asked. "Is there a Mrs. Earl in the picture?"

His eyes got big in mock protest. "Wow, you just get right to it, don't you?" he asked with a chuckle.

Bea started to apologize and hang her head, but then remembered she didn't have to do that around Travis. Instead, she lifted her chin high and met his eye contact. "Well, you know," she said. "Inquiring minds and all."

"I get it," he replied. "It's a reasonable question. And you can ask me anything." His hand was still on her shoulder. "The answer is no. There's no Mrs. Earl in my life. I've dated here and there, but it never turned into anything serious."

"Isn't that something?" Bea mused. "All these years, and you're still an eligible bachelor."

"I guess I haven't found *the one*," Travis said, moving his hand slowly around to the back of Bea's neck, underneath her long hair. "Although, there was the one who got away. I think you know her, actually."

This is escalating quickly, Bea thought to herself.

She was largely powerless when it came to Travis' charms. She knew she probably ought to feel guilty. She was a married woman, after all. Except she didn't. Her marriage was a sham. And the connection she and Travis shared felt true and good. It felt like they belonged together. It felt incredibly right.

"I might know a little something about that," Bea managed to say between heavy breaths. His touch was making her wild with desire.

"Tell me again why we couldn't be together," Travis prompted as he stepped closer, his lips less than an inch away from Bea's ear. Her knees buckled as she felt the heat coming off his body and smelled his familiar, sexy scent. "I mean, really together, Bea. Happily ever after together. I wasn't kidding when I said that I've been waiting for you."

"Don't be silly," Bea said, although she knew he was serious. She didn't move to step away. "I'd feel terrible if you've been pining for me all this time. You deserve better."

"Maybe," Travis said, sliding both of his hands around Bea's waist and lacing his fingers together in the small of her back. "But if I end up with the love of my life in the end, it will have all been worth it."

Bea was completely and totally taken with this man. Here he was— a decade after she had walked away from a future with him— professing his undying devotion. And she had chosen John Hughes, who resented her very existence.

What's the matter with me? I got it all wrong.

"Travis..." Bea began. "You're amazing and I'm flattered. But I came here to tell you something important. I think I should get to it. You might not feel the same about me when you hear what kind of trouble I'm in."

"Nonsense," he said, squaring his face against hers and moving to kiss her on the lips.

"I mean it," Bea said, pulling away. She didn't want to pull away. In fact, she wanted nothing more than to melt into his arms and make sweet, passionate love to him. But first, she needed Travis to know the truth.

"Okay, okay," he said. "Lay it on me."

14

"It started with a phone call. On the landline," Bea began. "Nobody even uses that anymore." She paced back and forth in the kitchen area of Travis' loft. He leaned back against the counter, his arms sprawled out beside him. The pose accentuated his muscular physique.

"Yeah," Travis affirmed in his gentle, everything-will-be-okay voice. "Take it slow or you'll wear a hole in my floorboards, babe. Tell me what happened."

"I was in my backyard studio," she began. "It's more of a shed, really. My sisters are right about that. But it makes me happy and John doesn't want paint in the house, so I use it to cope. To get my artistic talent out, you know? It has to come out of me somehow. Somewhere. Better an art shed than, well, I'm not sure. But it works."

Bea noticed how relaxed she felt around Travis. She could hear herself using more words and going into greater detail than she normally would. It reminded her of a time when she was allowed to be her true self. Without criticism or manipulation.

"Okay," he said, listening. "So you have a landline in your... shed?"

"That's right," she continued. "But nobody uses it. Anyway, it rang yesterday afternoon. And when I answered it, it was a robotic voice on the other end who said they knew what I had done. Can you believe that?"

"That's... Unsettling."

"And then some," Bea added. "I froze. I didn't know how to respond."

"That's understandable," Travis said. "A call like that would rattle anybody."

"Yeah, I guess," Bea said. "Perhaps the worst part is that I heard a click on the line and I'm pretty sure someone inside my house was listening."

"Who was home?" Travis asked, maintaining his posture. He seemed steady. Like he thought the problem could be handled. Bea was surprised.

"That's the thing," Bea said. "It could have been one of several people listening. Mom was there."

"Really?" Travis asked. "How is Lana doing? I always thought I'd like her."

"She's good," Bea said. "She's been living with us. Although she left for Natalie's last night. She will probably be there for a while. It may take me some time to get things sorted out."

"Last night?"

"I'll get around to that," Bea explained. "But I have to tell you about the afternoon first. When the phone call came in, Max was in the house, too."

"Max!" Travis exclaimed. "Such a good kid. What is he now? Thirteen? Fourteen?"

"He's fourteen. Just started high school," Bea answered. "He's a very good kid, if I do say so myself. He was hanging around and had just gotten home from school when the phone rang."

"Okay, well," Travis mused. "That doesn't sound so bad. Your mom and Max will be on your side. If it comes out about what happened, you can just tell them your side of the story. They'll believe you."

Bea appreciated Travis saying this. But it wasn't that simple. He didn't know everything. "I pray you're right," she said. "But it's more complicated than that. And besides, Ruth and Natalie had just arrived from Sacramento and were in the house as well. It could have been either one of them listening in."

"Ah, the Denton twins," Travis remarked. "Those two always sounded a little off to me."

"You don't know the half of it," Bea said. "But I can't speak badly about them. They did me a great kindness last night."

"Oh?"

"Yeah," Bea said. "I'll get to it. I guess there's more to tell you than I realized."

"For you," Travis replied. "I'd listen all day and all night, for as long as you want to talk. Take your time."

The way Travis treated Bea was bolstering her confidence. Deep down, she knew she deserved to be treated this way. She wanted to be adored.

"Are you sure you aren't needed downstairs?" Bea asked. "The showroom is open this time of day, right?"

"It is, but it's no problem. My assistant, Richie Barnes, will take care of any customers who come in. He's a good guy. I hired him a few years ago. One of the best business decisions I've ever made. You should meet him. He's heard a lot about you."

"I'd like that," Bea said, smiling. This was the easiest conversation she'd had with anyone besides Max in a long time. And to think it was about such an upsetting topic. Just goes to show that with the right person, everything seems better.

"So," Bea continued. "My mother, my son, and my sisters were all inside the house and anyone of them could have been listening on the line. For all I know, more than one of them was listening. And on top of that, John came home early, which he rarely does. He was in a mood, too. It made me wonder if he'd received a call at work."

The morning newspaper was sitting unopened on Travis' kitchen table. Bea wondered if John's tantrum last night had made it in before press time. She was tempted to look, but wasn't sure what good it would do in the grand scheme of things. Whatever they had written about him was deserved. Bea had little sympathy.

"Aw, babe," Travis said. He looked like he was resisting the urge to take Bea into his arms. "I'm sorry you had to go through that. I hate hearing it."

"Thank you," Bea said. It was so nice to talk to someone who cared. "Well," she continued. "Our neighbor lady acted damn strange, too. We were on our way out to dinner last night when she pulled her car in front of our SUV. John got out and the two of them had a heated discussion. Maybe I'm just paranoid, but it made me think they were talking about me and that they knew something."

"Okay," Travis said. "But I remember that night at Eagle's Point. I remember how shaken up you got when that guy took a tumble down that steep embankment. I admit, sometimes I think about him and wonder what happened. We probably should have called the authorities. But I understood why you didn't want to. A police report would have placed us together and would have been next to impossible to keep from John. But you did nothing wrong, Bea. Other than being with me."

"I wish that were true," Bea said.

"And I wish you didn't think being with me was wrong," Travis said quietly. "I wish you wanted to be with me for the rest of our lives. I wish you'd pick me. I've made no secret of my feelings for you."

"It isn't like that," Bea said. "There's more to the story. It's complicated."

"Then tell me what I'm missing."

Bea stopped and twirled a lock of her hair. She was thinking. She thought about how good it would feel to get this off her chest. But she was scared.

"What if I told you I had something to do with that man taking a tumble?" Bea asked reluctantly. Her tone was somber.

Travis reached out to Bea now and pulled her to him. He wrapped his arms tightly around her shoulders and held her against him securely. She could feel his heart beating in his chest. "Then I'd tell you I'm sure you had a good reason and that I love and support you no matter what."

15

"Hello? This is Bea," she said as she stepped away from Travis Earl and answered her mobile phone. She recognized the number as Max's school and so didn't want to let it go to voicemail. She had started to greet the caller with her full name, but felt self-conscious in front of Travis. She wished her last name wasn't Hughes.

It was Principal Maguire on the line and the news wasn't good. Max was in trouble. Bea's presence was requested at the school immediately.

"I'm on my way, but I'm down by the bay right now. It will take me about thirty minutes to get there," Bea said, then ended the call.

"Is everything alright?" Travis asked, genuine concern in his voice.

"I've got to go. It's Max. He's in some kind of trouble, which is completely out of character for him."

"Go," Travis said without hesitation. "We can finish this discussion later."

"Thank you," Bea said as she picked up her handbag and fished the rental car key out.

"Hey, I realize what I'm about to say might sound crazy," Travis began. "But what if I come with you?"

"What?" Bea asked.

When they'd been together before, she hadn't wanted Travis to be seen with her in public. She had been actively planning to leave John and was being extra careful in the hopes that her husband would be more generous when it came to matters of custody and visitation. She had been ready to go through with it and had made arrangements for herself and Max to stay in a small apartment just a few blocks down the street from where she stood, right here in Travis' loft. And then the incident happened at Eagle's Point, derailing her life. A man died that day at Bea's hands. Afterward, she was so shaken and so afraid of what she'd done that she couldn't face what she knew would be John's formidable wrath when he found out she was leaving him. And besides, she needed John's protection.

But things were very different now. Max was old enough to make clear his own wishes about custody and visitation. And last night at Honey Hog showed just how out-of-control John really is. His behavior took the situation from something Bea could keep private and convince herself wasn't that bad to a widely known and very public melodrama. In a way, John's outburst last night was a gift. It allowed Bea's mother, her sisters, and by now, probably anyone who cared to search John's name on the Internet to see what a maniacal tyrant he really was. Although Bea was still working to process it all, she felt less inclined to tuck Travis away and keep him a secret. Who would blame her for pairing up with a balanced, reasonable, and age-appropriate man? She suspected no one.

Another thought at the back of Bea's consciousness was hard to admit and bring into the light, but it was there. If she were about to be found out soon and arrested, she might as well squeeze every ounce of happiness out of her days before that happened.

"You know what?" Bea answered. "If you can get away, come on. Spend the day with me."

"Seriously?" Travis replied, looking as excited as a kid at Christmas. "I mean... Yes!"

Bea laughed at his enthusiasm. It felt good to be with Travis again and to see how much he cared for her.

"I'll be right there. Just you wait a few minutes," he said. "I need to run down and tell Richie I'll be gone."

"I'll wait in the car. Silver sedan with a rental company sticker on the back," Bea said, then she walked over and planted a warm kiss on Travis' lips. He stood up straight in response, leaning down over Bea and again wrapping his arms tightly around her body as he pushed against her and kissed her deeply.

"Babe," Travis said. "I think this might be the best day ever. I'm not sure I understand what brought this about, but I'm not complaining."

"Settle down now," Bea said, half teasing. "Like I said, I have a lot to fill you in on. You might not be so excited once you get your mind around what's happening with me. It's a lot. I'm a lot."

"Why don't you let me be the judge of that?" Travis said, smiling brightly as ever.

16

Travis put his hand on Bea's knee as she drove. And she let him. She marveled at the ball of emotions swirling around in her belly. She thought it almost felt like she was observing herself from a distance. Like she wasn't really there in her own skin. Good and bad moved around together inside of her as if they were old friends.

Travis continued to grin from ear to ear. Bea thought what he had said about this being the best day might actually be accurate from his perspective.

Had he really waited for me all these years?

It seemed almost too good to be true.

When they arrived at Max's school, Travis said he would stay in the car so as not to get in the way. He didn't want to be presumptuous when it came to Max. Bea could tell Travis had the proper perspective in that regard. She knew he wouldn't try to push himself on her son, no matter what ended up happening between the two of them romantically. He hadn't done it before and Bea was certain he'd handle things the same way this time around.

If there was to be a this time around. Bea still hadn't decided. But Travis' respect for boundaries was a relief. Bea had enough to tackle and didn't think she'd be able to bring anything else into the mix if it meant complicating life for Max.

The sun was climbing high in the sky and warming the day as Bea walked up the steps at the front of East Valley High School. Planters filled with colorful mums greeted her at the double doors, their blooms standing at the ready for the upcoming fall season. East Valley was a good school. And a friendly one. It had been so when Bea attended and she was glad the spirit of community continued now that her son was a student here. As she placed her hand on one of the large brass knobs to open the door, she tried to imagine what Max might have gotten himself involved in.

"Hello, there," a tall, brown-skinned lady said to welcome Bea. She looked the part of a high school teacher with her bouncing curls and rimmed glasses. Bea thought she was probably one of the nice teachers who went easy on the kids when they didn't finish their homework. She had always believed those teachers were the best kind. Being a kid was tough enough. A little extra kindness never hurt.

"Hi," Bea said cheerfully. "I don't believe we've met before. I'm Bea Hughes. Max's mother."

"Please to meet you, Bea. I'm Annie Rogers."

"The pleasure is all mine," Bea said. "I attended this high school many years ago, but my son is new. This is his freshman year. I'm eager to get to know all the fresh faces."

"One down and probably quite a few more faces to go," Annie said with a gentle laugh. "I suspect there have been a few new teachers added since you were a student here. Although you don't look a day over twenty-five."

Bea immediately liked Annie. She had a quiet confidence about her that made Bea feel safe. The kids probably felt the same way in her presence.

"You're too kind," Bea replied.

The halls were mostly empty, so Bea assumed it must have been the middle of a class period. She wondered if Annie had a planning block. Otherwise, why would she have left her classroom?

"I'm sure you know the way," Annie said. "But I'm heading to the office myself. How about we walk together?"

"That would be lovely," Bea replied.

Annie took the lead and Bea followed, marveling at how the inside of the school looked so different yet still the same. The office wasn't far from the front of the building, so it didn't take long to get there. Bea and Annie talked about the weather as they walked, remarking on how it would turn cooler soon.

When they arrived at the school office, Bea could see Max through the window on the top half of the door. He was sitting in a chair in an awkward position with his backpack strapped onto his back. His hair was a rumpled mess, and it looked like he had a gash on his forehead. His shoulders were hunched over. When his eyes met Bea's, Max looked reassured. He moved to embrace his mom, but caught himself, apparently realizing that might be an embarrassing choice for a young man of his age.

"Max!" Bea said as she walked towards her boy. "Sorry it took so long, but I came right away. What on Earth is going on? Are you hurt?"

"*Mom*," Max said simply, opening his eyes wide and gesturing across the waiting area to another boy who was also waiting, but with a sour expression on his face.

Bea stood in between Max and the other boy to shield her son from view so he could give her some idea what was happening. She lowered her eyebrows and pointed a thumb back towards the other kid. Meanwhile, Annie made her way to a desk on the other side of the room, which was staffed by a young, gangly man with a thin sprout of blonde hair. He looked nervous. Presumably, the young man was a receptionist or secretary. Bea hadn't met him before either.

"That kid is Landon Prater," Max mumbled, pulling Bea's attention back.

"And does he have something to do with why I was summoned here today?" Bea asked.

"Yeah," Max said. "He called us criminals."

"What?" Bea asked, perplexed. "Criminals? Who did he call criminals?"

How could this kid know anything about my crime? And who is this kid, anyway? He must be new in town.

"He said our family was nothing but white trash pretending to be important. And that we were common criminals. Then we got into a fight."

Bea turned and looked at the boy who maintained his sour expression. She tried to process what was going on.

What would make this Landon boy say such a thing? And why

*would Max care? He'd always been able to shrug taunts like that off.
It was odd for him to have taken it seriously.*

Bea turned back around to face her son. But before she could ask him anything else, the door to the principal's office shot open, and a harried, middle-aged Asian man stepped out.

"Mrs. Hughes, thanks for coming," he said as he reached out his hand to shake Bea's. "My name is Michael Cho. I'm the assistant principal here at East Valley High School. Glad to meet you."

"Hello," Bea said, shaking Michael's hand. She thought he seemed nice enough. She hoped the administrators wouldn't be too hard on Max given what was happening with his home life. They probably didn't realize he had spent last night in a hotel room instead of his own.

"Come on in," Michael said, motioning to the inside of the principal's office. "The others are waiting."

"Okay," Bea said. She wanted to ask which others he was referring to, but she decided to wait since she knew she would probably find out momentarily.

"Boys," Michael added in a serious tone, lowering his head as he addressed Max and Landon. "You stay here for now. We'll call you in when we're ready for you."

Bea turned and gave a look of comfort to Max, then followed along behind Michael Cho. Her muscles tightened as she stepped into the office and saw her husband seated in one of the wingback chairs. Across from John sat an official-looking lady Bea presumed was Principal Maguire.

Dammit. What is he doing here?

Bea tried not to react.

"Hi, Mrs. Hughes," the lady said as she stood up and reached out to shake Bea's hand. "I'm Jenny Maguire, the principal here. Vice Principal Cho and I appreciate you and your husband coming in."

Maybe they don't know anything is wrong between us.

"Have a seat," Michael prompted.

Bea hadn't expected to see John. He looked haggard. He was dressed in a business suit, like usual, so had apparently been at the office this morning. His appearance was rough around the edges though. His tie was loosened just a little too much and his shoelaces were knotted haphazardly. Stress was taking a toll on him. Bea wondered what the town council's reaction to last night's meltdown had been. Surely, his colleagues knew about it. He stared straight ahead without acknowledging his wife, so Bea didn't attempt to make eye contact. Instead, she focused her attention on Jenny and Michael, eager to hear what they had to say.

"What's happened?" John asked. Bea could tell by his forceful tone that he would take over, like usual. "You said it was important."

Bea willed herself to speak. "Yes, let's get right down to it."

Michael looked at Jenny, deferring to her. He raised his chin as he stood behind her like a sentry.

"Alright," Jenny began. "I appreciate you both coming in. I understand this is a stressful time for your family."

"Oh?" Bea said. Even though she knew exactly what Jenny was referring to, she didn't want to admit it right off the bat.

"We know about last night," Jenny said. "And the kids do, too. It's all over the Internet. Today, Max experienced some blowback."

"Look," John said without hesitating. "I take full responsibility for my behavior." Bea recognized the political-speak. John was a master at schmoozing. Leave it to him to somehow talk his way out of this. "In fact," he continued. "I'm holding a press conference at Town Hall this evening during which I will publicly apologize. My wife will be there by my side and together, we will put to rest any rumors that may be circulating."

Bea's face suddenly felt hot.

What the hell was John talking about? Did he really have the nerve to make a proclamation about me being by his side? How presumptuous.

"Then you're aware that a number of rumors are floating around?" Jenny asked.

Now Bea and John looked at each other. As they did, she saw a glimmer of compassion in her husband's eyes. She knew he loved his son.

"What rumors, specifically, are you referring to?" Bea asked.

Now it was Jenny and Michael's turn to look at each other again. Michael took in a deep breath, held it, and then let it out with a heavy sigh. He pulled a chair over and sat down, then slowly crossed one leg over top of the other.

"Well, what is it?" John asked.

Jenny leaned forward and put her elbows on the desk. "If you don't already know, I'm not sure how to tell you. Have either of you been on the Internet this morning?"

"No," Bea said. "I purposely avoided it. Max and I... We spent the night in a hotel last night and I've had other matters to attend to. I knew videos from our dinner at Honey Hog would make their rounds. But I didn't think there was anything I could do about it, so I didn't bother to look. Experiencing the evening live and in person was quite enough."

Jenny shifted her gaze to John.

"I haven't been online either," he said. "I spent the morning discussing my situation with colleagues. We needed to come up with a strategy to handle the hit to my image. And, of course, to make things right with the owners of the restaurant."

"So you're serious?" Michael asked, inserting himself for the first time. "You really don't know?"

The burning sensation spread from Bea's face down her arms and to the ends of her fingertips, which began to tingle. At any moment, things could fall completely apart.

Was this the moment?

"Just tell us already," Bea said, the words toppling out of her mouth faster than she would have liked.

"Show them," Michael said to Jenny.

Reluctantly, Jenny moved her hands to the keyboard that sat at rest in front of her computer. She quietly went through the motions of typing her password to gain access to the machine, then entering some keywords to find what she was looking for. It took less than a minute to get the video queued up and ready. As she turned the monitor around for John and Bea to view, the room went silent. You could have cut the tension with a knife.

"Play it," John said, gripping the arms of his chair like

an airplane passenger experiencing significant turbulence for the first time. Bea shook her head up and down as confirmation. She was as ready as she'd ever be.

As the black screen turned to color and began to move, a shadowy figure wearing a hoodie and a face mask came into view. It was impossible to tell whether it was a man or a woman, young or old. The figure spoke in a robotic voice just like the one Bea had heard on the telephone. For emphasis, words appeared on the screen as they were spoken.

"Rosemary Run's mayor, John Hughes, has a secret. His wife killed a man in cold blood and he's helping her cover it up."

17

"Ludicrous," John said as he stood up and began to pace at the back of the room. "Is this some kind of joke?"

Jenny and Michael looked at each other yet again. They were trying to figure out how to handle the Hughes family's situation with as little impact to the school community as possible. That was their job and Bea knew it, but she found herself unable to speak. The room spun around her as she began sweating profusely and gasping for air. Suddenly, her windpipe felt like it had been put in a vice. She started shaking like a leaf, her entire body convulsing. She told herself to stop it and to get it together, but those imperatives did no good. Bea's body continued in a frightening downward spiral as a sense of impending doom settled over her. A relentless tightness filled her chest. It felt like an elephant had slammed itself down right on top of her. Bea raised a hand to the place where it was most uncomfortable, her heart galloping hard as if every beat was a struggle. She thought it might decide to pound right out of her chest.

"Mrs. Hughes," Michael said gently. "Can I bring you a glass of water? You aren't looking so good."

Bea grabbed onto Michael's arm and nodded her head yes, her eyes wide and wild with terror. "It hurts," she said feebly, clutching a spot near her breast bone.

"She could be having a heart attack," Jenny said to her assistant. "Get the school nurse, would you, please?"

"Sure thing," Michael said quickly as he left the room.

"And ask Annie to take the boys back to class while you're at it. We will speak with them later," she called after him. "We don't want to alarm Max, so keep things low key."

"Got it," Michael confirmed hastily.

"Max..." Bea mouthed, tears flowing down her cheeks. Nothing but a gasping sound came out.

Jenny moved fast, grabbing a brown paper bag out of her desk drawer filled with what looked to be her lunch, then dumping the contents out and rushing to Bea with the bag. "Here, breathe into this," she instructed. "Breathe as deeply as you can. All the way into the lowest place in your belly. You'll want to engage your diaphragm."

Bea took the bag, smashing it to her face clumsily while John continued to move around the back of the room. "Come on, Beatrice," he scolded. "Cut it out. Someone wants to get a rise out of us. And you're playing right into their hands."

"Respectfully, Mr. Hughes," Jenny asserted. "Back off and give her a minute."

With Jenny's permission as a small comfort, Bea

continued to descend into what seemed like a dark abyss. The feeling of being outside of herself grew stronger as scenes from the night of the incident flashed through her distressed mind. She threw herself to the floor of Jenny's office, though the change of position was barely perceptible from her perspective. In her head, she was back at Eagle's Point on that fateful night. She could see the wretched man so clearly as he lie on the dirt, his body convulsing much like her own. His short, brown hair was stained with blood where the indentation on his skull was visible. Bea had thought his head looked like a jack-o'-lantern, smashed by rowdy teenagers at Halloween. She hadn't known what kind of damage a baseball bat would do. She hadn't taken the time to consider it before she'd swung wide and with all her might.

In an instant, everything went black.

18

W hen Bea came to, she saw several sets of feet in front of her face, positioned sideways. It took her a minute to figure out she was on her side, splayed out on the floor of Principal Maguire's office. She noticed two sets of feet wearing matching shoes and moving towards her. As Bea raised her eyes to follow the shoes upwards past the matching black pants and crisp, white uniform shirts, she realized that a pair of officials were here to take her away.

"No!" she said to them as forcefully as she could manage. "I can't go! My son..."

"Take it easy, Mrs. Hughes," Jenny said from somewhere in the distance. "You're going to the hospital to get checked out. We'll take good care of Max while you're gone."

"That's right," one of the uniformed officials said. His voice seemed like it was coming from somewhere in the distance, too. "We're EMTs. We're going to help you. Try to relax."

Relax? They want me to relax?

"I've got Max. Don't worry. Let the professionals take care of you," said a genial voice. Surprisingly, it belonged to John. Bea thought maybe she was imagining things, but he sounded... kind. Whatever had happened, it must have spooked him. His tone reminded her of the old days when they had first met. It soothed her and made her feel safe. She knew it would be fleeting and was mostly an act, but she clung to any small bit of support she could come by these days.

Bea smiled slightly, then rolled onto her back. She tried to relax her shoulders. She knew she needed help. She decided she should get checked out. She would let the EMTs do their job and help her. She cooperated as they scooted her onto a backboard. She was calming down and the pain in her chest was starting to subside. Until her thoughts turned to Travis.

Travis!

No sooner did she think about Travis than he burst through the doorway, a look of grave concern on his face. "Babe!" he exclaimed through watery eyes. "Are you okay? What happened to you?"

Bea felt whatever color was left drain from her face. Her mouth fell open. She was at a complete and total loss for words. "I... I'm..." she tried.

Travis rushed to her side, kneeling down in an open spot beside one of the medics. He grabbed Bea's hand and lifted it up to his lips to kiss. "I'm right here," he said. "And I'm not going anywhere."

Bea could feel John's eyes on her. And she could predict what he would say before the words came out of his mouth. He'd try to keep himself under control since there was an audience present, then he'd let Bea have it later.

"Beatrice," John began. "How about you introduce me to your friend?"

The room became so quiet you could hear a pin drop. The male medic glanced down at Bea's wedding ring, then at Travis' left hand and finally at John's. Bea felt ashamed. So much so, that she wished she were invisible. She wished she could sink down into the floor and remain hidden underneath. She thought about how sad her life had become. She'd known things would unravel one day, but this wasn't how she'd pictured it.

"Oh," Travis said, releasing Bea's hand and getting back onto his feet. "John Hughes, I don't believe we've met. I didn't see you over there."

Travis didn't reach out his hand to shake John's. He was polite, but he intended to stand his ground. His confidence made Bea both grateful and nervous. She was desperate for someone to love her so much that they would stand up for her in the face of any challenge. But on the other hand, she was petrified about what might transpire with Travis and John in the same room. Especially since Travis had called her babe.

"How do you two know each other?" John asked, crossing his hands at the front of his waist in what looked to Bea like his typical politician posture. Everything John did seemed to irritate her these days. She was beyond fed up with him.

"We're old friends," Travis said, glancing at Bea. She supposed that description was as good as any.

"Let me get this straight," John said, his temper rising. "The two of you are old friends who just happened to be together the morning after my wife and son spent the night at a hotel instead of at our home. I doubt I'm the only one who thinks that seems a little suspicious."

"More like we're old friends who can count on each other to be there when things get tough," Travis replied, standing up straight and puffing his chest in a primal show of physical dominance. Bea didn't think she had ever seen Travis this upset. He was an easy-going guy who was slow to anger. But not today.

"I see," John said sullenly. "You're old friends who call each other babe."

"John!" Bea whelped. The sound that came out of her was more like a squeak than a voice. The pain in her chest was easing up, but bad feelings were rising towards her neck, determined to force their way out somehow. She thought she might vomit.

When Travis heard Bea's pitiful response, he stepped in front of her, placing himself between her and John.

"Let me guess," John began. "You think my wife needs protected... From me."

"I don't know," Travis responded, looking around the room at the medics and Jenny for a show of support. "Does she?"

The tension in the room was becoming nearly unbearable. The medics continued to check Bea and get her properly strapped down onto the backboard, but she could tell they didn't want to be in the middle of any of this. Jenny seemed to want to stay out of it, too, but Bea got the idea that Jenny felt bad for her. Bea thought they were all wondering if John would lose his cool like he had the night before at Honey Hog.

"Mrs. Hughes," Jenny said as she stepped close to Bea and placed a hand on her forearm. "Is there anyone you can talk to? A professional, I mean."

Bea shook her head no, but the thought of it and what a relief it would be sent a flood of tears pouring out of her eyes. She wanted so badly to confess what she had done. She needed to get it off her chest. Holding it in was hurting her and turning her life to shambles. Bea began to sob. Big, fat tears rolled down her cheeks, her body heaving as the emotion forced its way out of her.

"I'm sorry," Bea said quietly to Jenny. "I don't know what's the matter with me. Things are jumbled up. I don't know what to do to make them right."

Jenny reached over and got a notepad and pen from the top of her desk. "Here," she said as she jotted down a name and number. "This is a friend of mine who is a psychologist. His name is Martin Duffie. He was trained at Yale and is one of the best. I'll tell him to expect your call. I think he could really help you."

Travis turned away from John and squatted down on the other side of Bea. "Babe," he said. "I think she's got the right idea here. Once they check you out at the hospital and clear you to leave, let's call Dr. Duffie. I'll wait with you and will drive you wherever you need to go. I won't leave your side."

Bea was mortified that John was hearing all of this, but the doting felt good coming from Travis. She was realizing that she had been deprived of love and affection for so long that she craved it. She needed it. She felt guilty for needing it, but she did. She couldn't help it. She was only human, after all.

Tears continued to roll out of Bea's eyes. It was as if a fountain had been turned on and the flow couldn't be stopped. Wetness soaked the sides of Bea's hair and the backboard below her. She had needed a good cry for a long time. Because John had always been so quick to tell her to suck it up, she had made a habit of holding her emotions in. She had even come to believe crying was too messy. A show of weakness. But holding her emotions in wasn't working, that much was clear. Here she was, in front of Travis and relative strangers, crying her eyes out.

"Babe," Travis tried again, his voice gentle and soothing. His confidence in calling her babe in front of John was impressive. But before Travis could finish, Max burst through the door with Michael Cho and Annie Rogers following closely behind him.

"Mom!" Max exclaimed as he threw his backpack down and rushed to his mother's side. "Are you okay?"

Travis stood and took a step back.

"She's fine, son," John said while standing still. He didn't move towards Max. "She got herself worked up. You know how she is. Nothing to be too concerned about."

Travis and Jenny shot John the same disgusted look while Max ignored him.

Hadn't John shown a glimmer of kindness just a few minutes ago?

"Really?" Travis asked John sarcastically, unable to stop himself.

"I'm okay," Bea said, finding her voice while

embracing her son. "They're going to take me to get checked out by a doctor. But I think I'm fine."

"I'm sorry," Michael said to Bea. "Annie and I tried to stop him. We were almost back to his classroom when Max saw the ambulance parked outside and thought it might be here for you."

"I'm not sure how he even knew to think it a possibility," Annie added with a chuckle. She seemed impressed by Max. "Your son broke into a sprint and we couldn't keep up. I don't blame him. I probably would have done the same to get to my mama."

Jenny gave a sympathetic look to her colleagues. She wasn't upset with them and she wanted them to know it.

"It's understandable that you'd be worried about your mom," Jenny said to Max. Then to Michael and Annie, "Don't worry. Max Hughes is where he needs to be."

"Thank you," Bea whispered. "Thank you, all."

There was a moment of silence as Bea and Max held each other and everyone else looked on, touched by the love between this mother and son. The two of them had a connection that other people wished for. It was a bond that could not be broken. Not by school bullies, not by John, and not even by a physical separation should Bea be arrested. Deep down, Bea knew she and her son would remain close no matter what happened. Her relationship with Max was the best part of her life.

Suddenly, Max noticed Travis.

"Who's this?" Max asked. His expression was one of curiosity. It almost seemed like he recognized Travis.

Could he remember? It was such a long time ago. He was so little.

The adults in the room looked at each other, unsure how to answer. Travis smiled, a look of excitement on his face. He was eager to be officially introduced to Max now that the boy was older. He wanted both Max and Bea to be a prominent and permanent part of his life.

"I'm Travis. Travis Earl. Pleased to meet you, Max." Travis extended his hand towards the boy.

"Hello," Max said politely to Travis. Then he turned to Bea. "Mom, have I met this guy before? He looks familiar."

Bea's eyes grew wide as she contemplated the best response. For years, she had worried about exactly what Max had seen the night of the incident. She had wondered if it would negatively affect him. She had wondered if it would mess him up. That was the last thing she wanted. Even if Max hadn't seen Bea hit the man in the head with a baseball bat, he had certainly experienced terror that night. They say kids are resilient. But they also say childhood trauma can have adverse effects that last for an entire lifetime. Bea cursed the vile man who had brought trauma to her son's childhood. *Damn him.*

At several points, Bea had thought about taking her son to see a child psychologist. Every sign that hinted at a potential issue with Max's development had thrust Bea into a panic. Common childhood occurrences like wetting the bed once in a while or pretending to talk like a baby had caused Bea great concern. In fact, she would have taken Max to a psychologist if she hadn't feared what he might report. She had ultimately decided taking him to see someone was too risky.

In place of seeking professional help, Bea had done

her own research on child development. She knew she wasn't qualified to really help Max, not like a professional could, anyway. But she figured she'd learn and do her best. It was another thing she had spent her time on while John was at work and Max was at school. Just like the letters and videos she created and stashed in the attic in the event of her arrest. Based on everything she'd read, she thought Max was doing okay. But even after years of research, her knowledge was limited. At least she felt like she was doing something.

A myriad of potential issues flash through Bea's mind as Max looked at her expectantly. The statistics for children of divorce were troubling. And the same for children of a mentally ill parent. Would she and John split up? Would she be diagnosed with a mental illness given her apparent inability to handle the stress? The statistics for children who'd had an incarcerated parent were the worst of all.

"Travis owns a furniture store down by the bay," Bea said, trying to put the rest out of her mind.

"Yeah, I build the furniture myself," Travis added proudly.

"That might be why he looks familiar, Max," Bea said. "We bought some furniture he made when you were little. Our big dining room table and several side tables in the house are from Travis' store. Maybe you remember going with me when I picked them out."

"Right!" Travis said, more excited now.

Max nodded his understanding as he continued to sort through memories. He squinted his eyes and put one hand on his chin as he thought.

The mood in the room was still tense, but Bea thought maybe they were over the hump and that she would get through her school visit without any major upsets beyond what had already happened. She let out a deep breath she had been holding and relaxed back onto the board beneath her as the medics finished their final preparations to transport her to the hospital. They were moving slowly, which Bea took as a good sign.

Max stood beside his mother and seemed content with her explanation until suddenly his jaw dropped and he looked like he might cry. Bea turned to see what he was looking at. To her horror, John was rushing Travis from behind, one arm positioned to wrap around his unsuspecting neck.

J ohn's attack landed on the back of Travis' head with a thud. He gave it all he could.

"You bastard!" John yelled as the force of his weight knocked Travis off his feet and took him to the ground. "It all makes sense now. You were sleeping with my wife! *Are* sleeping with my wife! How dare you? Who the hell do you think you are?" He sounded like a madman, ranting as he flailed around.

Travis was younger, bigger, and stronger. John probably wouldn't have mounted an attack face on. Coming from the back and using the element of surprise was the only way for John to have gotten a leg up on his formidable opponent. As the two of them hit the floor together, John used his fists to pommel the back of Travis' head. Disoriented, Travis looked around to get his bearings. "Hey now, John!" he shouted. "Take it easy." It was obvious Travis never expected John to make such a bold move. But it only took a minute for Travis to turn the tables.

In what looked like an effortless maneuver, Travis reached one arm around, wrapping it across John's back. Then using his other arm and his toes to lift himself off the ground with John still on his back, he flipped over, causing John to lose his grip. Travis had moves like a wrestler. He was agile and limber. Even when it looked like he was pinned and at a disadvantage, he knew exactly how to pivot to regain control. John was sent flying backwards while Travis sprung to his feet.

"Dad!" Max cried. "Why are you doing this? You're scaring me."

Max's face was stoic, even as the emotion threatened to burst out at the seams. He was doing his best to handle the disturbance like a young man instead of a boy. Bea was at a loss for words, but she pulled her son to her and held him as he cried, the young man giving in to the force of his feelings. Bea had been afraid of what might happen with her two beaus in the same room, but was still surprised to see this skirmish taking place. She had hoped things wouldn't get any crazier.

The male medic pulled a radio from his belt and called for police backup. He didn't wait to ask before doing so, which was unnerving for Bea. It felt like things were happening around her she couldn't control. Like an inevitable chain of events had been set in place that— for better or worse— had to play themselves out. She hated what John was doing to Travis. She hated what he was doing to their family. She just wanted peace in her life.

Is that really too much to ask?

Travis went silent and Bea couldn't get a read on him.

She wasn't sure if he was angry or whether he just felt sorry for John. She had never seen Travis in this type of predicament, so she wasn't sure how he would react. He held the power. He could have returned John's attack and easily beaten the older man. But so far, it looked like he was only defending himself, careful not to injure his adversary in the process. Bea appreciated the example Travis was setting for Max. If her son couldn't count on his dad to keep it together, at least he was witnessing a good man who could.

John, on the other hand, was coming unglued. His volatility was increasing. He apparently wasn't able to control his temper anymore. Bea wasn't sure what was going on with him, but she decided right then and there that she and Max would not stick around to figure it out. A small part of Bea appreciated the fact that John was feeling protective of her and jealous of Travis. But he had been so cold and distant for so many years that it was too little, too late. Not to mention, this wasn't the right way to show it.

Time seemed to slow as a flurry of activity happened in the school office. Jenny, Michael, and Annie positioned themselves in different parts of the room as if they were breaking up a juvenile fight in the cafeteria. They stood, arms crossed or hands on hips, and made it clear they weren't going to allow this melodrama on their watch. John retreated to the other side of the room, where he continued to shout insults about Travis and Bea as he licked his wounds. Apparently, he had injured his back during the onslaught because he was hunched over and holding onto it. Max continued to cry. All while the medics finished their job of getting Bea prepped for transport. She didn't want to let go of Max, but the medics insisted there was no room for him to ride in the back of the ambulance with her to the hospital. Jenny promised to see to it that Max was taken care of.

"Who can I call?" Jenny asked.

"Mom!" Max pleaded. "I want to go with you!"

"I'm so sorry, son," Bea said tearfully. She hardly had the energy to explain. Something was happening to her physically, although she didn't understand what.

Jenny told the medics to wait a minute, then went to her computer and pulled up Max's emergency contact information. "Lana Denton is listed here first. Your grandmother, right, Max?"

"Grandma is out of town," Max cried. "I want to go with my mom."

"He's right," Bea added. "My mother is in Sacramento with my sisters today… After what happened last night." Bea didn't bother to look at John as she said it. She tried to tune out his presence and pretend like he wasn't even in the room. She wished he wasn't in the room.

"Don't worry," Jenny said, talking quickly to settle arrangements before Bea had to leave. "How about Gabrielle Radnor? I see her listed here as a family friend."

"Yes!" Bea confirmed, louder than anything else she'd said. "Gabby is my best friend. Max will be safe with her. She'll come right away to pick him up."

Max was satisfied with that decision. He had grown up thinking of Gabby as an honorary aunt. He knew she'd take good care of him. Besides, Gabby was confident and assertive when she needed to be. Max knew he wouldn't have to watch over her like he did his mom. She was more than capable of taking care of herself. Although he couldn't articulate the differences, he looked forward to Gabby's involvement in his family's situation. Maybe she would know what to do to get them out of this mess. "Okay," Max said to Bea. "I'll be okay with Aunt Gabby."

"Good, then it's settled," Jenny confirmed. She stood and walked over to put her arm around Max's shoulders. She knew the police would arrive any minute to deal with John, and she wanted the boy to feel supported. It had been a difficult few days for him. As Jenny bid goodbye to Bea, she leaned down and gave her a warning.

"Mrs. Hughes," Jenny began. "I want you to know something. When I played that video, I was looking right at your husband. He wasn't surprised to hear what the hooded figure had to say."

"What?" Bea asked, confused.

"I'm telling you, I saw John's face," Jenny repeated, whispering so Max wouldn't hear. "Your husband already knew. Be safe, please. You could be in danger. And call Dr. Duffie for advice, will you?"

Bea promised she would as the medics lifted her onto a wheeled stretcher, then rolled her out of the building. She was relieved to be leaving the chaotic scene in the office until, to her shock, she emerged through the double doors to find that a small crowd had gathered in front of the school. Bea didn't recognize any of their faces, but their presence made her heart pound. A few of them were holding up smartphones, taking her photo and recording video.

What are they doing here? Do they know? Does everyone know?

As the sunshine hit her face and the breeze lifted strands of her dark hair, Bea's senses began to dull. She suddenly grew sleepy and out of sorts. Once again, everything went black.

20

The man behind the robotic voice smiled as he stood casually in the parking lot of East Valley High School and watched Bea Hughes be taken away in an ambulance. He had just treated himself to a nice ham and egg breakfast at Lorraine's Diner and was feeling extra proud of himself that day. He held his smartphone up high and without an ounce of shame as he recorded the scene. Thanks to his extensive IT expertise, he knew no one could positively identify him. He'd include this footage in his next video.

He had toyed with the idea of using a Guy Fawkes mask, when he appeared on camera, like the hacktivist group known as Anonymous. He admired the group's boldness and refusal to cave on their principals. But he hadn't wanted to steal their thunder or anger them by being a copycat, so he'd opted for a simple hoodie overtop a black ski mask with low lighting and a voice changer. It did the trick. Besides, he wasn't the one committing a crime. At least not yet.

He was a good guy. A whistleblower. He was bringing a wrong to light. And when it benefitted him personally, even better. He knew he wouldn't get the praise he deserved from the public. But he could live with obscurity for the time being. It was too important that he remain anonymous if he wanted to accomplish his ultimate goal.

He felt pleased with himself that a tweet from the new account he'd created had been enough to gather a crowd of this size in the small town of Rosemary Run during the middle of a workday. He did a quick headcount and determined that thirty-three people stood with him. That made thirty-four including himself and thirty-six if he counted the medics. *Thirty-eight*, he thought as a police car arrived on the scene driven by Officer James Tatum. A young female deputy rode in the passenger seat. He made a note to learn her name. He might want to use it.

For a moment, he closed his eyes and imagined what it would feel like once this was all over and he got everything he wanted. He'd been waiting for so long. He thought about how it wasn't fair that John and Bea Hughes lived an enchanted life in the public eye, complete with a big, beautiful house and a doting son. He wanted what they had. He wanted to live in that big house on the hill. He wanted to be in the public eye, admired by the town's people. He even wanted to be a parent. In his early forties, he was tired of waiting for his life to begin. He was tired of being told he had to stay in the shadows and that he wasn't good enough to be brought out into the light because of what he was. Because of what *they* were.

Now, finally, he was taking matters into his own hands.

21

When Bea came to this time, she found herself in a hospital room. A clock ticked quietly on the wall and an IV machine hummed gently beside her. The light was low in the sky, barely visible out the window. Bea panicked.

"How long was I out?" she asked, to no one in particular.

"I don't know for sure," Lana replied from the other side of the bed. "But I suspect it's been six or seven hours. The nurse said they'd given you a sedative."

Bea startled. "Mom? What are you doing here?"

"My girl is in the hospital. Where else would I be?"

Bea smiled, but her head throbbed when she moved to sit up too quickly. "Ouch," she mumbled. "So... how did you get here?"

"I borrowed Natalie's car and drove. Lean back and rest," Lana instructed. "You've had a tough time of it lately."

Bea did as she was told. She didn't want to

inconvenience Lana, but was glad she was here. It was silly, but Bea had always wanted her mom when she wasn't feeling well.

Berryhill Community Medical Center was located in a neighboring town near the bay and Travis' furniture shop. The last time Bea had been here, her dad was sick. She had successfully avoided the place ever since, even opting for a home birth when Max made his entrance into the world. She remembered that the views out every window were stunning, but they didn't make up for the sad memories being in the building brought back. Even the smells went through Bea like lightning rods, returning her to painful times. She closed her eyes and breathed deeply to get her bearings.

A pretty Latina nurse with her hair cut into a stylish bob noticed Bea was awake and came in to check on her. Her name tag read *Susana Herrera*. "Hi, there," she said as she pumped a handful of sanitizer into her palm from the dispenser on the wall by the door. "How are you feeling?"

Susana was fit and perky. Her curls bounced as she walked. Bea thought she looked like the picture of health in every way. Susana's physical presence was a contrast to the rundown shell of her old self that Bea had become. She knew her eyes were sunken and her hair brittle. She had lost weight and muscle tone due to the stress she'd been under. It had happened slowly, so she could sort of pretend it wasn't as bad as it actually was. But she knew the difference. Travis must have seen it, too, yet he had complimented her.

"I'm good. I think," Bea replied.

Susana chuckled. "I know you're still waking up. No rush. You're doing great."

"Thanks," Bea replied, basking in the praise. She was such a ball of insecurity. She hated it.

"Do you remember what happened?" Susana asked.

It took Bea a minute. She was still disoriented.

"Principal Maguire said you were at Max's school, remember?" Lana prompted. "She called me."

"Oh, yeah. *Max!*"

"He's fine," Lana said reassuringly. "He's at Gabby's."

"Right."

"Is Max your son?" Susana asked politely as she changed the bag of saline attached to Bea's IV. She seemed at ease, chatting while she worked. Bea figured patients loved Susana just like the kids at school loved Annie. Bea thought it must feel good to be liked and appreciated.

"Yes," Bea confirmed. "He's fourteen. My one and only. He was there when the ambulance picked me up. I hated for him to see his mother like this."

"Don't be so hard on yourself," Lana said to her daughter. "You're a wonderful mom. I think it's time you cut yourself some slack."

Susana smiled and winked at Lana. "I'll bet you're onto something there. As they say, mother knows best." She laughed heartily and wrinkled up her nose.

There was a knock on the door and a pale-skinned, balding doctor entered. His eyes were bright and he appeared intelligent, but he looked sad. In fact, Bea could feel the sadness emanating from this man without even having to look at him. She thought about how it must be difficult to practice medicine day in and day out, especially considering all the bad things that happen to people. It must be disheartening to realize you can't save everyone.

"Beatrice Hughes?" the doctor asked, pushing his rimless glasses up the bridge of his nose with one finger.

"That's me," Bea said timidly. She felt weaker than she sounded.

"Pleased to meet you. I'm Dr. Ronald Benjamin. I'll be taking care of you." Dr. Benjamin got a handful of sanitizer from the same pump Susana had a few minutes earlier, then pulled a stool over and sat down beside Bea's bed. He smelled like the distinctive scent of hospital soap. Perhaps he had just scrubbed up after surgery or a patient procedure. The aroma poked into Bea's lungs like a knife. Another reminder of her dad's health troubles and heartbreaking death.

"Nice to meet you, too," Bea replied as she worked to collect herself. "What's going on with me, doc? I think I passed out. Before that my chest was hurting."

"I don't know for sure yet, but I promise you we will find out," the doctor assured. "It's my job to get to the bottom of this."

Lana was concerned, and it was evident in her face. "Do you think there could be something wrong with my daughter's heart?" she asked eagerly. "I don't want to jump to any conclusions, but her father had congestive heart failure before he died. I can't help but worry she might have a genetic predisposition to heart trouble."

"Wow," Bea said, fiddling with a wad of the hospital blanket and feeling helpless. "I hadn't even thought about that. Do you think there could be something seriously wrong? Like there was with Dad?"

"Let's not get ahead of ourselves," Dr. Benjamin said. His voice was calming, and Bea appreciated his bedside manner. A quick glance at Susana confirmed that she admired Doc Benjamin and felt the same way. Her trust helped put Bea at ease. "I want to run some tests," the doctor continued. "We'll start with an EKG and a stress test. If we find any irregularities, then we'll adjust our plan and go from there."

Bea cringed at the thought of being hooked up to an EKG machine. She couldn't imagine needing such a test. *Weren't those for old people?* She thought of herself as entirely too young and healthy to even be discussing the possibility, as if she had strayed from the lane in life where she belonged. Things were getting jumbled and happening out of order.

"Neither test is a big deal," Dr. Benjamin added, sensing Bea's reluctance. "Neither one is invasive or even uncomfortable, aside from any fatigue you may feel while walking on a treadmill. The technicians are trained to watch your reaction closely. They won't push you too hard. I promise."

"Two promises in less than five minutes," Bea said with a chuckle, attempting to lighten the mood. "I hope you're a man of your word, Dr. Benjamin."

The doctor tapped an index finger on a clipboard he was holding and smiled. He was thinking.

"I can assure you he is a man of his word," Susana said convincingly. "You're in good hands, Mrs. Hughes."

Bea smiled back at Dr. Benjamin, then at Susana, and

finally at her mom. Bea was apprehensive, but felt like she was in good hands. However, she wasn't convinced that feeling would last. There was so much to untangle in her life. The sedative was wearing off and Bea was becoming more and more lucid. As she did, she felt the strong urge to confess her crimes to a compassionate listener. The words were bubbling up and resting on the tip of her tongue, desperate to be spoken. Maybe she could tell the people right here in this room. What was the worst that could happen if she did? Bea's face suddenly felt hot as she remembered the video. She wondered if Dr. Benjamin and Susana had seen it.

Dr. Benjamin reached out and placed his thumb and one finger on Bea's wrist, feeling for her pulse. "Is something upsetting you now?" he asked. "Your face is flush and your heart rate has gone up in the time we've been talking." He turned to Susana and asked her to get a monitor, then opened his clipboard and scribbled down some notes.

"I'm okay," Bea said feebly.

"Are you concerned about the tests?" Dr. Benjamin asked. "Because if you need me to, I can give you something to calm your nerves."

Bea was tempted by the offer of medication to calm her. Many times in the years since the incident at Eagle's Point, she had considered turning to alcohol or drugs to numb her pain and ease her anxiety. But she never had. She knew that doing so would be a slippery slope and she couldn't have done that to Max. The last thing he needed was a drug-addicted mother. No, she'd hold the anxiety in as best she could so as not to hurt anyone else.

After all, she'd caused enough pain and suffering for an entire lifetime when she pushed that man over the edge of the hill. She shuddered to think what his family must have gone through. That is, if he'd had a family. She'd spent countless sleepless nights thinking about them, imagining their despair when he disappeared without a trace. As far as Bea knew, his remains had never been found.

"No, I don't want to take anything I don't have to," Bea said. "My heart races from time to time. I'm used to it. Maybe I can just do some deep breathing. It will slow down again." She took a few long, deep breaths to demonstrate.

Lana reached out and put a hand on her daughter's shoulder. It was a nice gesture and one that provided Bea comfort. Meanwhile, Dr. Benjamin scooted his stool closer against the side of the bed and looked intently into Bea's eyes. "Mrs. Hughes?"

"Please, call me Bea."

"Okay, Bea. Do you often find yourself feeling anxious?"

"Maybe," Bea said. "I'm no medical professional. I'm not sure what to watch for."

"Are you under a lot of stress in your life?"

Bea hesitated.

"I can answer that one," Lana said. "She most certainly is. I'd say her stress levels are through the roof."

Bea shrugged her shoulders and looked down at the blanket she continued to trace and twirl with her fingers. It was soft, woven out of threads dyed the color of wheat. It reminded her of one she'd had as a kid, back when life was simple and the worst thing she had to worry about was being picked on by her older sisters.

Dr. Benjamin lowered his voice and tried again. "Is there anyone you can talk to?"

Bea didn't answer right away, so Lana did. "My daughter is a pretty private person," she began. "I've lived with Bea and her family for the past few years. I've known she struggled, but I didn't come to understand the full extent of it until the past couple of days."

A fresh wave of nausea moved through Bea as she heard her mother's words.

Had Mom been the one listening on the line yesterday when the call came in?

Bea didn't know how her mother would react if she found out the truth. Lana was kind and loyal, and she had always been supportive of her daughters. But she was also an honest person with strong morals. Bea thought it possible that her mother would march her down to the police station and force her to turn herself in once she found out what she had done. And a part of Bea thought such a scenario might be a relief.

Dr. Benjamin glanced at Susana, then raised one hand and smoothed the tiny hairs on the back of his bald head. "Look, Bea, I'll be frank," he continued. "I know that your husband is the mayor of Rosemary Run. And I'm aware of both the disturbance at the restaurant last night and the accusations being directed at the two of you. That's a lot for anyone to handle."

Ashamed, Bea tucked her chin tight against her chest and pulled the blanket around her shoulders. A single tear fell from her eye. She wanted nothing more than to be invisible in that moment.

How did this become my life?

"It's okay, dear," Lana said, patting Bea's shoulder. "None of that is your fault."

Oh, but it is.

Sensing Bea's need for more support, Susana pulled up a chair on the other side of the bed and placed a hand on Bea's knee. Dr. Benjamin turned his attention to Lana.

"You're Bea's mother?"

"Yes, I'm Lana Denton," she replied. "Pleased to meet you."

"Thank you for that insight, Ms. Denton."

"You may call me Lana. And you're welcome. I want the best for my daughter. I don't want to interfere if it might cause trouble, but she seems to think she has to handle everything alone. We all need a hand sometimes."

Bea sat frozen in place. She felt like she was in a trance. She couldn't look at them anymore. If she spoke, she might blurt out her confession.

Doctors had a duty to report things like murder confessions, right?

Once the words were spoken, Bea knew she'd soon be taken away. She wouldn't see Max again outside of prison walls for many years. She couldn't do that to him. She had to hold it together. Not to mention, if there was something wrong with her, she needed treatment. Even worse than leaving Max while she went to prison would be leaving him permanently if her own life came to an untimely end.

"You know what," Dr. Benjamin said. "I have a few things I'd like to check on before we continue this discussion." He gave Susana a look as he said it and they both stood to leave the room. "Ms. Herrera and I will be back later. Lana, talk with your daughter, please. Let's see if we can do something to alleviate some of her stress."

"When can I go home?" Bea blurted, surprising herself with the strength in her voice. It sounded like it had come from outside of her. "Or at least, back to the hotel I'm staying at?"

"I'm not sure yet," the doctor said, sighing. His compassion was sincere. "But I want to keep you overnight. Settle in for at least that long. I'll see you again soon. I'm on duty all evening."

With quick movements, Dr. Benjamin and Susana shuffled out of the room, leaving Bea and her mother alone.

22

"Beatrice Elisabeth Hughes," Lana said when the door closed. Bea remained in her position, chin tucked, frozen in place. She didn't dare look at her mother. She knew what was coming next. "I know what you've done."

Was Mom the caller? No. She couldn't have been. Could she? She must have been the one listening in.

Time seemed to stand still as the nausea gained a stronghold in Bea's body. She could feel hot vomit rising in her throat like molten lava, insisting she expel it. Just in the nick of time, she grabbed a plastic bowl from the tray beside her bed and retched into it. She hated being so weak. She cursed her body for failing her, yet again. At this rate, she'd have to carry barf bags around with her on a regular basis.

Neither mother nor daughter spoke a word for what felt like an eternity. Lana was waiting, and her silence made it clear she had the patience to do so for as long as it took. Bea stood and made her way to the bathroom to get herself cleaned up and empty the plastic bowl. She stalled as long as she possibly could until finally, she gathered the strength to face her mother and take part in what she knew would be one of the most important discussions of her entire life. Bea returned to her bed, tucked the sheet and blanket back in neatly at her sides, then lifted her head as high as she could in a show of confidence. She might as well try and act confident. There was no escape.

"So, you heard?"

"Yes, I did."

Bea winced. Her mother wouldn't make this easy. At least not yet. "I heard a click and thought someone in the house was listening in. I'm just glad it wasn't Max."

"No, it wasn't him," Lana confirmed. "He was in the living room with me. I was looking right at him when the call came in. The same goes for your sisters. They were there, but I was the only one who picked up the phone." Lana maintained a neutral expression. It reminded Bea of when she had been in trouble as a young girl. Lana and Freddy had been fair parents. Bea hoped that her mother would be fair now.

"That's quite a relief," Bea said. "This whole thing is worrisome enough without thinking my fourteen-year-old son overheard."

Lana nodded without saying anything else.

"Did you hear about the video that's circulating, too?" Bea asked. "Apparently, the same person has posted it online using the same robotic voice to disguise their identity."

"I did," Lana said. "Myra actually called to tell me about it. I felt like a switchboard operator this afternoon with all the calls coming in and going out."

Bea chuckled. It might have been an inappropriate time, but it felt good to break the tension. It would feel even better to confess. "Well, what do you want me to say?"

"I think the real question might be about what you want to tell me." Lana posed to her daughter. "I'm ready whenever you are."

Bea leaned her head back against the pillow and weaved her hands together on her chest over her heart. "Fine," she said. "But you may never look at me the same. Are you prepared for that possibility?"

Lana scooted to the edge of her chair, then reached a hand out to stroke the top of Bea's head, her familiar perfume wafting through the air. "You're my child," Lana said emphatically. "Nothing you say and nothing you have done will change that. I can see how this is tearing you up inside. It's okay to let it out. It's just us. Your mama is here."

Bea wanted to cry; she was so moved by her mother's words. But her body seemed like it was short circuiting and doing all the wrong things at the wrong times. No tears would come. The words of her confession were still on the tip of her tongue, but they felt heavier now that they were ready to be said.

"Go ahead," Lana prompted, still stroking her daughter's hair.

"Something happened," Bea began. "I did something. A bad thing."

"When did you do this thing?"

"Almost ten years ago now. Max was just four-years-old. He was with me." Bea stared at the television mounted to the wall in front of her while she spoke, as if doing so would somehow give her story a happy ending. She needed something to anchor her.

"In Rosemary Run?" Lana asked.

"Nearby," Bea answered. "It was at Eagle's Point, just over the ridge. At the Overlook there. I was... well, Max and I weren't there alone."

"Okay," Lana said softly. Bea thought maybe her mom had already guessed what was coming next. Lana knew that her daughter's marriage was in shambles.

Bea took a deep breath before she continued. "I was seeing someone... Romantically. I had been unfaithful to John. I was planning to leave him, actually. I had arrangements in place to rent an apartment for me and Max. I was all set to go through with it, too."

Lana didn't hesitate. "Bea, honey, that's understandable. I've seen firsthand what John can be like. I think he's a good man at heart, but something is wrong between the two of you. Don't be so hard on yourself for wanting better," she said sympathetically.

"I appreciate that, Mom," Bea said. "But if I hadn't been there sneaking around with Travis, none of it would have ever happened. I can't shake the feeling that I'm being punished. Instant karma. And the punishment keeps coming." She shook her head at the thought.

"Travis? Is that the friend of yours who builds furniture?"

"That's the one," Bea confirmed. "He's a great guy. He's a much better match for me than John, in all honesty. And he treats me wonderfully. He always has."

"Aw, my dear girl."

"I know," Bea said. "I saw him this morning for the first time in many years. He was as nice as ever. And he's still single."

Lana smiled and then raised her eyebrows. She was excited at the thought of a man who would treat her daughter right.

"I know," Bea repeated. "It's really nice. But that's beside the point. The night it happened, Travis and I just wanted to see each other, so we met up and talked while Max played on the playground at the Overlook. Max was little enough that he didn't notice anything unusual about our relationship. We kept things strictly platonic when he was around. But the evening went bad and took a life-altering turn."

"Tell me, dear," Lana prompted again. Bea needed a lot of coaxing, but Lana didn't mind.

Bea wiped her eyes as if she had been crying, although still, no tears would fall. "It's hard to say it out loud," she admitted. "No one else knows. At least, that's what I thought until I got the phone call yesterday morning." Bea broke away from staring at the TV and turned to make eye contact with her mother as she mustered the nerve to speak her truth. "I hit a man in the head with a baseball bat. I watched him fall to the ground as his body convulsed and blood poured from the back of his wound. He landed a mere few feet away from a steep drop off. It pains me to say this, but in a panic, I pushed his body over the edge."

Lana gasped as the confession took the air out of her lungs. "Oh, my," she said. "Did Max… ?"

"He didn't see," Bea said, already feeling lighter after

sharing her burden. "At least, I don't think so. I had him in his car seat with one of the buckles snapped. I'd had to buckle him in hastily, but I don't think he could turn all the way around. The man and I... We were behind the minivan."

"And Travis?"

"That's the thing. He wasn't nearby when it happened. He had walked to the other side of the parking lot to get something out of his truck. By the time he returned, it was all over."

"Did you ever tell him?"

"No," Bea said. "But after that night, I broke things off with Travis and halted my plans to leave John. I was scared to death and shaken up by what I'd done. I believed I needed John's protection. He'd always felt sort of like a father figure to me, you know? I hate to say it, but it's true."

"I can see that," Lana affirmed. "But Travis... Didn't he find it strange that you suddenly ended things? He was probably heartbroken. And are you absolutely sure he didn't witness what happened? Could he be the anonymous caller? Maybe it's a ploy to get you back."

"I don't know. He did seem happy to see me again and eager to be in my life after all this time. Travis was with me when I received the call this morning to come to Max's school, so he rode along. I'm not sure what you've heard, but it turned into a huge mess in the principal's office, complete with John attacking Travis from behind and trying to choke him out. Travis is a lot younger and in much better shape, so needless to say, that didn't go very well for John."

Lana and her daughter laughed together. They couldn't help it. It was as if their bodies needed a way to release some tension.

"Mom, you're being awfully nice about all this. I have to admit, it's not what I expected."

"Bea, I've known for a long time that you were wrestling with something big. Sometimes when we don't know the truth, our imaginations get carried away and we come up with possibilities that are even worse than reality. You have no idea the range of things that have gone through my mind."

"But I killed a man. It's horrible. There's no greater sin. It's been excruciatingly difficult to live with myself. If it weren't for Max, I would have already turned myself in."

Lana stood up and had Bea scoot over, then she climbed into bed beside her daughter, wrapping her arms tightly around her. "Bea, my darling, you are a good person. I know that about you without any shadow of a doubt. I know it like I know my own name that there's more to this story, and that you had a good reason or you never would have done it."

Now the tears came, forceful and fast, as they ran down Bea's face and onto the sheets below. She didn't deserve this kindness.

"That's almost exactly what Travis said earlier when I tried to tell him," Bea mumbled between sobs. "Why do the two of you believe in me? You don't even know why I did it."

"Because we don't have to know why you did it," Lana said. "We know *you*. And that's more than enough."

Bea put one hand over both of her eyes as she continued to cry hard. She hadn't known what her mother's reaction would be, but she was so incredibly glad to be confessing to her now. She had carried this burden alone for so long. It was heavy. It was long past time to lay it down, one way or another.

"I'm here for you," Lana said. "I know it's difficult to relive and put into words. But I'd like to know what happened that caused you to do it. Will you tell me?"

Bea nodded her head, then used a few tissues from the nightstand beside her bed to dry her eyes. "The whole thing was traumatic," she said. "I'm not sure if you can get PTSD from something like what happened to me and Max, but if so, I feel like I might have it. It has affected me in the most horrible ways. I'm not the same person I was prior to that day."

"Go ahead," Lana urged. "Let it out. You'll feel better once you do."

"Okay," Bea replied. "Here it comes. Like I said, Travis had gone to the other side of the parking lot to get something out of his truck. The sun had just set, and it was getting dark outside. We were almost ready to head home, but Max had to go to the bathroom. He was still at the age where he couldn't have been expected to wait for a long time once he said he had to go. It had only been a couple of months since he had turned four." Bea let out a deep sigh before continuing. It was painful for her to explain and painful for her mother to hear. "The place was nearly empty, with just a few cars left. The bathrooms were housed in a small cinder-block structure near the overlook. The men's restroom was on one side and the women's on the other, divided by a single wall and a water fountain near the entrances. I didn't think anyone else was around, so when Max asked if he could go in the men's room by himself like a big boy, I said yes thinking nothing of it. I filled my water bottle and enjoyed the view of the pink evening sky while I waited."

"Oh, no," Lana said.

"I knew it would take Max a little while. Every part of the bathroom process was still clumsy for him. Not to mention, he was a happy little guy and often took his time, looking around and sort of playing as he went. He'd never encountered anything scary or truly dangerous. He was young and innocent at that time, depending on his parents and the other adults in his life to keep him from harm."

"Oh, Bea," Lana said as she held her daughter and leaned her head gently against the back of one of her shoulders. "I think I know where this is going, and it's making me sick to my stomach."

"Around the same time I began to suspect something was wrong," Bea continued. "I heard the deadbolt on the inside of the men's room door latch. I ran to it, praying that I'd heard wrong. The deadbolt was high on the door. There was no way Max could have reached it to turn the lock himself."

"My God," Lana said, squeezing her daughter tighter and tighter, tears forming in her eyes.

Bea was emotional, but she was committed to telling the story now. It was like ripping a scab off. Even though it was painful, she was determined to finish the job. It would bleed, but once started, it had to be finished.

"When I reached the door, I slammed into it with my

whole body, but it wouldn't budge. It was locked tight. I yelled Max's name and began to bang on the door. For an excruciating few seconds, I heard nothing. The world seemed to have been thrust into slow motion. I wasn't sure what was happening, but every fiber of my being told me that what we were encountering was danger of the highest order. I trusted my instincts to tell me what to do. I was ready for a fight. I didn't have time to feel scared or to even think about hesitating. I had to get to Max."

"Of course. How terribly frightening. Horrifying, really!"

"As I banged on the door harder and louder, I heard Max calling for me. He sounded alarmed, but not terrified. I took it as a good sign and hoped he had not yet been hurt. But I knew I couldn't wait. I had to get into that men's room. My minivan was parked nearby, so I ran to it, rifled through the back, and pulled out the only thing I had that could be used as a weapon: a wooden baseball bat. My mind was flooded with sickening scenes. I'd heard about the kinds of things that happen to little kids when child predators get their hands on them. I didn't think I had time to call for help. As darkness descended, the place had cleared out. There wasn't anyone within earshot. I didn't think Travis would be able to hear me, so I saved my energy and focused on handling the danger myself."

"Bea, I'm so sorry you had to go through such horror. And alone, no less. I had no idea your secret was anything like this. No parent should have to experience what you did."

"I've never been more scared in my entire life," Bea added. "It may sound strange, but as I walked back towards the bathroom with the bat in my hand, I talked to Daddy and asked him for help." Bea began to cry a fresh round of tears as she remembered. "I looked up at the heavens and I asked my daddy to help me save my boy. I told him I didn't know how any of that worked or whether he could actually lend his help, but I told him I needed him more than ever."

"Oh, my dear," Lana said through her own tears. "I don't know how any of that works either, but I know your daddy loved you so much. He would have loved Max just the same. He had always looked forward to becoming a grandfather. And if he could have helped in any way at all that day, I know he would have." Lana sobbed now, too. "Oh, my sweet girl. And our sweet, innocent little boy. Tell me the rest of the story."

Bea continued, eager to get to the end. Her confession was almost done. "As I approached the bathroom," she explained. "I saw a man walking towards me. Everything about him was revolting for some reason. I'm telling you, I had a visceral reaction to the sight of him like I've never experienced before. He looked deranged. At minimum, he was mentally ill, but I suspect he was also some kind of addict. He had short, brown hair and a long, narrow face. His neck seemed somehow too long, almost like depictions of aliens I've seen. The vile man was holding a young boy over his shoulder. There was a delay as I worked to process what was happening, because the child was wearing different clothes than Max had been that day. When the man saw me, he didn't flinch. In fact, he appeared to strengthen his resolve. He leaned his head forward on his knobby neck and began to walk quickly towards an old Volkswagen bus that was idling nearby. The boy he was carrying faced the opposite direction over the man's shoulder until suddenly, the child turned around and looked at me. It was our Max."

Bea paused and blotted her eyes some more as tears rolled down her mother's face. She took another deep breath, then continued.

"It was then that I truly realized the urgency of the situation. This man had waited in the bathroom for a child to prey on. And he'd had the wherewithal to immediately change the child's clothing, thereby changing his appearance. That was a disturbing level of premeditation. We were dealing with a sicko bent on taking Max and doing God knows what with him. I rushed forward and, for some reason, I thought about wolves and how they go for the Achilles when they want to take out another animal. They know that if an animal can't run away, defeating them becomes much easier. As I reached the man, I used the baseball bat to swing hard at his knees. I was hell-bent on stopping him from taking Max away. The man yelled out in pain and fell to the ground, releasing his grip on my son. From that point on, everything became a blur. Max ran to me. I remember scooping him up and holding him so tight. He leaned his little head down on my shoulder, unsure of what was happening but glad to be back in the safety of my arms. Still acting on instinct, I put Max into his car seat and like I explained earlier, I buckled one of the buckles. I was in a hurry, because I needed to get back and deal with the man before he got away, or worse, came after Max again."

"Damn right you did," Lana added. It was unusual for her to use such strong language.

"Even though it was all a blur, I was aware I was making a decision at that juncture. I could have gotten in my van and driven away. The man had been wounded and probably wouldn't have been hard to find. I could have gone to Travis and together we could have called the police. Travis might have even been able to hold him until police arrived. But something inside me insisted that wasn't an option. I knew I couldn't leave him be. I didn't know his history, but I knew I was in the presence of true evil. It made my blood run cold. I couldn't leave that man free to snatch another child. When Max was secure, I closed the door to the van and walked to the back where the man was crouched on the ground, still holding onto his knees. It may have been a coincidence, but the wind began to whip up as I stood there. It blew leaves off the trees and created a rustling sound that echoed through the canyon below. I didn't bother to approach the man from the front or to look him in the eye. He didn't deserve that courtesy. I approached from behind, lifting the bat high and hitting it onto the back of his head as hard as I could."

"Wow."

"You have to understand, Mom," Bea explained. "This man had his hands on my child. During the time they were locked in the bathroom together, I know for sure that he changed Max's clothes. I don't know if he touched Max inappropriately or did anything else that traumatized him. I wasn't going to wait around and let a man like that go. Maybe it was the motherly instinct inside of me. I did what I felt was right and finally, the harrowing incident reached its crescendo. In a mix of determination and panic, I pushed and kicked the man's body, rolling him over the side of the hill. He barely made a sound as he tumbled down the steep drop-off to the rocky landing below."

There. Bea had said it all. It was out of her and spoken into the ether, a burden now shared by her mother.

What in the hell do we do now?

23

L ana and Bea were still holding onto each other, Bea gently blotting her eyes, when Susana Herrera returned.

"Miss Bea," she said in her cheerful, sing-song voice. "You have a visitor. Is it okay for him to come in?"

"Really?" Bea asked. She hoped it was Travis. Now that she'd told her mom what had happened, she wanted to finish telling Travis, too. Maybe the three of them could come up with a plan together. Plus, now that she had some time to reflect on it, she was touched by the way he had stood up for her at the school office. She wanted to thank him.

"Really," Susana confirmed. "He's eager to see you."

"Good! Send him in."

Lana moved back to the chair as Bea propped herself up in the bed and did her best to smooth down the disobedient strands of hair which had become disheveled from laying down. Lana had never met Travis before and

Bea looked forward to introducing the two of them. A meeting was long overdue.

Susana left the room. When she returned, it wasn't Travis she escorted in. To Bea's great disappointment, it was John.

"Here he is," Susana announced happily, not understanding the implications.

"Hello, Beatrice," John said in a dry voice. "And Lana."

Susana exited the room again, closing the door behind her this time. Poor Susana. She was only trying to help.

Just great, Bea thought to herself.

"I assumed you'd be in jail by now," Bea said to her husband.

John stood at the end of Bea's hospital bed with his feet shoulder width apart and his hands crossed in front of his waist. It was the same peculiar stance he'd had in the school office earlier. It struck Bea as fake and pretentious. "No, I'm not in jail," he said sullenly. "Would you like me to be?"

"That's not what I'm saying," Bea replied. "Don't put words into my mouth, John Hughes. I'm not in the mood to fight with you."

"Well, you seem to be feeling feisty this evening. What's gotten into you?"

Lana bit her lip. Bea could tell her mother had a lot to say to John, but she would be respectful. John turned his attention to his mother-in-law. "Lana, would you mind giving me a few minutes alone with Beatrice?"

Lana turned to her daughter for the okay. "It's alright,

Mom," Bea said. "Maybe you could find us some warm coffee?"

"Fine," Lana said as she stood up and shuffled out of the room. "Shall I bring back three cups? Or just two?" she called back.

"Just two," Bea said. "John isn't staying." Being assertive felt good.

When the door closed behind Lana, and Bea and her husband were alone, his demeanor changed. He sat down in the chair Lana had occupied and dropped the good-guy act. "We have a problem," he said.

"Is it Max?" Bea asked, the concern evident in her voice. She didn't want to sound weak, but the thought of something being wrong with her son pushed her in that direction.

"No, he's fine, as far as I know," John clarified. "This isn't about him. At least, not directly."

"Okay, then what is it? Because if you'll notice, I have my own problems right now. You haven't even asked me how I am."

"Sure, you're right," John said in a rare admission. "I trust you're feeling better now and that you're going to be okay." He didn't reach out and touch Bea. Their relationship no longer had that kind of warmth. The only time John touched his wife anymore was in public when other people were watching. And even then, it didn't happen often.

"They're running some tests," Bea explained. "They're checking out my heart to be safe, but I sort of doubt it's anything serious. I've been under a lot of stress lately, and I know stress takes a toll on the body. Maybe I'll get lucky and the doctor will order me to a weekend at the spa."

John laughed, so Bea did, too. Things felt different between them. Bea felt like she had crossed a line from which there was no going back. Seeing Travis and telling her mother what she'd done had been freeing. Regardless of how things turned out, she was feeling less trapped by John and her secret. At least, for the moment. She was well aware how life could turn again on a dime. But she began to think perhaps she and John could be friends.

"We could all use a prescription like that," John said. "But seriously. I need to talk to you about something."

"Okay," Bea said. "You have my attention. What is it?"

John leaned forward with his elbows on his knees and laced his fingers together. "There's no easy way to say this, so I'll come right out with it."

"You're frightening me now, John," Bea said.

"I know," he said. He looked down at the floor as he spoke.

"What do you know? That you're frightening me?"

"I know *everything*."

"What in the world are you talking about?" Bea asked. Her heart began to pound again and she could feel her face getting hot.

"The video," John clarified. "The murder you committed and the accusation that I've been helping you cover it up. It's all true."

Bea thought she would vomit again, although she didn't know if there was anything left in her stomach. "I don't understand," she said. "In Principal Maguire's office, you said it was just someone trying to get a rise out of us."

"What else could I say with the others there?"

"But…"

"You can cut the bullshit, Beatrice," John said, his voice on the edge of nasty. "I'm telling you I know *everything*. I was there the night it happened."

Bea couldn't tell if he was serious or just trying to bait her for information. She had to be very careful. For all she knew, John was trying to gather information that could be used to blackmail her and keep her under his control.

"Are you recording this conversation?" Bea asked, out of nowhere. The thought had just struck her. She didn't know who to trust.

"What?" John asked.

"You heard me. Are you recording this conversation?"

"No," John replied. "That's not what this is about. I'm just as guilty as you are of withholding this information. Like it or not, we're in this mess together. Why would I record a conversation that implicates me?"

Bea's mind felt cloudy and her thoughts scattered. This was the last thing she had expected. If John had been there that night, why hadn't he stepped in to help? More importantly, why hadn't he mentioned it all these years? "I'm not sure what to say," Bea replied.

"Then hear me out," John continued. "I was there that night at Eagle's Point because I had followed you. I suspected you were seeing someone, and I wanted to know if I was right."

"John… I…"

He held his hand up to stop Bea. "That's beside the

point right now. I followed you in a colleague's car so you wouldn't recognize me. I watched as you and the man I now know to be Travis pushed Max on the swings and looked adoringly at each other. And then I saw... The rest."

"You mean...? I'm sorry," Bea said. "This is a lot to take in." She hated herself for apologizing.

Keep it together.

"I mean, *everything*," John continued. "I saw you run frantically to the van and get the baseball bat out of the back. I wasn't sure what you were doing, but then I saw the man. I didn't recognize the boy at first until he turned and I realized it was our son." John looked pained as he said the words.

"I didn't know what to do," Bea pleaded. "Truly, I did the best I could under the circumstances. There wasn't much time. I had to act. The risk of not doing anything and allowing Max to be taken away was too great..."

"I know. And I've never been prouder of you than I was on that day."

Bea thought she saw tears forming in John's eyes. She was floored. "You were *proud* of me?"

"Yes," John said. "Very proud. You saved our son. And for that, I will always be grateful."

"Wow," Bea said. "I wasn't expecting this. So you saw the whole thing?"

"I did. When I realized it was Max, I'd gotten out of my car and was on my way to intervene. But then I saw you put Max in his car seat and go back to finish the job. Maybe I panicked, but I returned to my car at that point, just in time to see you heave the man over the edge before I drove away. I would have done the same thing."

The camaraderie between Bea and John was something she had never dreamed possible. She was incredibly relieved to find out that not only did he know, but he thought she had done the right thing. But she didn't understand why he'd been so cold to her all these years. He'd acted like he resented her. If he knew what she had done and was proud of her, then what could explain his attitude?

"Thank you for saying that," Bea said softly. "It means more to me than you know."

John reached out and put one hand on top of Bea's. There wasn't an electricity when they touched like there was between her and Travis, but John's hand felt familiar and comforting nonetheless. He kept it there and patted Bea's hand a few times before withdrawing and laying his hands in his own lap. "So now that we've cleared the air, we have to figure out what to do."

"Right," Bea agreed. "But wait a minute," she said as she considered the situation further. "If you were there and saw what happened, how do I know you didn't orchestrate this yourself? How do I know you aren't the disguised man in the video?"

"Don't be silly," John sneered, his voice going back to defensive and adversarial.

"I'm serious, John," Bea said. "I know you haven't been happy with me for some time. Maybe you'd like to see me arrested and put behind bars to get me out of the way."

"Dammit, Beatrice," John said, slapping his palms on

his thighs. "There's a lot about me that you just don't understand."

"Then help me understand," Bea said. "You scold me almost every day like I'm your child instead of your wife. You rarely show me any affection and I can't even remember the last time we made love. I thought maybe it was me. I know I'm getting older and my career has stalled. I guess I wouldn't blame you if you were more interested in one of the young, pretty career women you interact with through your job."

John leaned back in his chair and looked up at the ceiling. Bea thought he suddenly looked haggard and frail. He was getting older, too, and signs of aging were happening much quicker for him than they were for her.

"This isn't the time or place to get into all of that," John said. "Right now, we need to work together to figure out what to do. We need to figure out who made the video and silence them if we want to hold our lives and our family together."

Although she would have liked to have known more about her husband's feelings towards her, she agreed that they had work to do. "Okay, I get it," Bea said. "I know you love Max. I don't actually think you would want his mother sent away. And if you did, you could have just told one of your friends on the police force instead of going through all this trouble. Let's get down to business. What are we going to do?"

24

B ea and John were talking like old friends when Lana returned, balancing two cups of coffee in her hands. John sat up straight in his chair when she entered, his body becoming rigid.

"Relax, John," Bea said. "Mom knows."

"You mean, *she knows*? How… ?"

"I told her a little while ago. Before you got here."

Now Lana was the one surprised. "Bea, dear, do you mean you told John the same thing you told me?"

"I didn't have to," Bea said. "He was there and saw it all with his own eyes. We were just talking about how we should handle our current predicament. Come on in and join us."

John raised his eyebrows, then quickly tilted his head to one side and nodded his approval. "I don't suppose there's any harm in the three of us working on this together now that we're all aware of what happened. We are family, right?"

"Good," Bea said, taking the coffee from her mother.

"Then it's settled. Mom, pull up a chair." But Bea could tell her mom had something else on her mind. "What is it?"

Lana looked hesitant as she sat down and got herself situated. She went ahead anyway. "I was just thinking about, well, the other person who was there that night. Shouldn't he be involved in this discussion?"

"You're referring to Travis," John said.

"Yes," Lana replied.

"I'm not so sure that's a good idea," John explained. "And not just because of what happened earlier. By the way, Travis chose not to press charges. My emotions got the better of me. But I realize he's not a bad guy. That was gracious on his part."

"Then what?" Bea asked. "I agree with Mom that it's probably a good idea to get him in on this."

John hesitated before he spoke more. "I'm not making an accusation here, but let's stop and think about the possibility that Travis is the one behind the video," John said. "We know he was there that night. And he has motive."

"What motive is that?" Bea asked, indignant. "Like you said yourself, John. Travis is not a bad guy. And you're absolutely right. I've known him for a long time. I can't see him being behind this. No way."

"Beatrice, his motive is you. Plain and simple."

Bea didn't want to hear this. It seemed difficult to trust herself these days, and she didn't want to doubt Travis. But she had apparently made the wrong call about John. Here she had thought he didn't care about her, and now she finds out that he was protecting her by not turning her in to the police.

Could that mean I was wrong about Travis, too? Could he be capable of doing something like this?

"I really don't think he would…" Bea mumbled as she absentmindedly fiddled with another section of her blanket.

"There have been threats directed at me," John said.

"What kind of threats?" Bea asked, concerned.

Lana wrung her hands as a worried look settled over her face. "I hope this situation won't lead to any more violence," she said. "People can get crazy. Mob mentality takes over faster than most of us would imagine."

"No threats of violence yet," John assured. "But I'm being blackmailed. It began with a letter sent by mail and received at my office yesterday morning. That's why Officer Tatum stopped by the house. He and I have worked together closely in the past, and so he was giving me the courtesy of handling the matter discreetly."

"What did the letter say?" Bea asked, alarmed now and worried for her family.

"It said I should resign from my office as mayor or else they would take your secret public. I thought they were bluffing. The letter didn't specify what the secret was, so I assumed it wasn't a big deal. A hoax, probably. Until yesterday afternoon when I received a call on my private line from someone using a voice changer."

Bea and Lana looked at each other knowingly. "I got one of those at the house, too," Bea said. "Yesterday morning. Mom happened to pick up the phone at the same time and overheard on the other end of the line.

That's what prompted me to tell her what happened at Eagle's Point."

"Huh," John muttered.

"Is it safe to assume that's what put you in such a foul mood last night at the restaurant?" Lana said to John. Her tone surprised Bea.

"I deserve that," John said. "I guess I cracked under the pressure. Can the two of you ever forgive me?"

"I think an apology would be nice," Lana added. "Under the circumstances."

John smirked, but not in a bad way. "Yeah, I'm sorry," he said.

Lana smiled and nodded, pleased with herself. Bea smiled at her mother's handiwork. She looked out the window as she ruminated on everything that had been said. The sun was low in the sky and nearly ready to disappear until the morning.

"Look, John," Bea said once she'd gathered her thoughts. "I don't mean to make light of this, but I've been living with the fear of being found out for an entire decade. Today, I finally got some relief. But I'm exhausted, both physically and mentally. I'm waiting on my doctor to come back in. He said he was checking on a few things in his efforts to figure out whether there's something wrong with me. And I'd really want to get some rest. Can we talk more about this another time? I don't think the situation will come to a head immediately. Do you?"

John looked at his wife and Bea thought that for once, he might have really seen her. "The two of us are supposed to be at a press conference in half an hour," John said. "As a public figure, I'm held to a different standard. You know how it works. The people of Rosemary Run want an explanation. I'm not sure how long I can put them off."

"Then go," Bea said. "You can still make it to Town Hall if you leave now. Just tell them your wife isn't feeling well. I'm not sure if you realized it, but there was a crowd in the school parking lot today when I was taken away in the ambulance. Many were taking pictures or recording video on their smartphones. I'm sure the people of Rosemary Run already know something is going on with me."

"I agree, but it may look suspicious, like you got sick once you'd been found out."

"And I trust you can handle the situation," Bea said. "You're a gifted politician. You can spin the story in such a way that you come out looking like the good guy, as usual. Just promise me you won't lie about what I've done. Avoid the truth all you want, but I can't live with any more lies. My heart can't take it."

John stood up and took Bea's hand into both of his. "Okay, I'll go," he agreed. "We'll talk again tomorrow. And in the meantime, please consider what I said about Travis. Maybe he wants me out of the picture, thinking it will clear the way for the two of you to be together. Good men have done plenty worse in the name of love."

25

B ea dozed on and off for the rest of the evening, her body completely drained from everything she'd been through. Dr. Benjamin and Susana came back to check on her, but when they saw how well she was resting, they opted to let her be, promising to return in the morning to discuss next steps. Several text messages came in from Travis, but Bea was too tired to respond. She opted to leave them ignored while she gained some strength and thought about what John had said.

Max called just before nine o'clock to say goodnight from Gabby's. He seemed to be in good spirits and was prepared to return to school in time for the first bell tomorrow. Once Bea had spoken to her son, she settled in for a good night's sleep. By the time she woke up bright and early the next morning, she had come to a decision. She wanted to keep her family together.

"Mom," she said to Lana, who was next to her on a cot. Susana had apparently brought it in while Bea was asleep. "Mom, wake up."

"What, dear?" Lana asked, still groggy. "Can't an old lady get any sleep around here?" They both laughed.

Bea found it odd, but she wasn't so afraid of being arrested anymore, even when that threat was more real than ever. Now that she realized how John had protected her, she figured he would do anything necessary to do it again. Between the two of them, they would work together to keep their son safe and their family intact.

Bea's direction was clear. She'd have to cut contact with Travis again. It would be hard. Being around him was so pleasant and the attraction between the two of them so strong. But her decision to stick with John had been the right one. They were in this together. After all, no one would fight for a child like his own parents.

"I want you to know," Bea began. "I've decided to stay with John. After our talk last night, it feels like the right decision."

"Oh, dear," Lana said, rising into a sitting position and swinging her legs around the side of the cot. She could reach the shades from where she was sitting, so she turned and opened them, allowing morning light to stream in and flood the room.

"What?" Bea asked. "You don't think it's the right decision?"

"I don't know," Lana said reluctantly. "It's not my decision to make. But I'll support you, no matter what."

"I appreciate that, Mom. I have a feeling I'll need your support. There's more ground to cover before this is all over and settled."

There was a knock on the door and Dr. Benjamin and Susana came in, both of them looking tired.

"Good morning," Susana said. Her voice wasn't as upbeat as before.

"You're still here?" Bea asked. "Do the two of you ever sleep?"

Dr. Benjamin cracked a slight smile as he rolled a stool next to Bea's bed and sat down. "We try to sleep now and then," he said. "We're heading home to get some sleep soon. But we wanted to talk with you before we left. How are you feeling this morning? You look a lot more relaxed.

"I'm good," Bea replied. "Much better than yesterday."

"That's great to hear," the doctor replied. He got out his stethoscope and listened to Bea's heart. "Any chest pain or tightness?"

"No," she replied.

"How about dizziness? Nausea? Feeling faint?"

"Not since last night."

"Good," Susana said as she again changed the bag of saline attached to Bea's IV. Both Susana and Dr. Benjamin were moving quickly this morning, probably eager to get their rounds done and hand things off to the staff taking the next shift.

Dr. Benjamin stepped back, returning his stethoscope to the pocket of his white lab coat. "I'm going to order those tests we discussed, along with some blood work. If everything looks good, you can go home around noon. I want you to follow up with your primary care doctor and maybe a cardiologist, depending on what we find."

"Okay," Bea said. "I can do that."

"I'll go ahead and tell you though," he continued. "I'm fairly certain you have tachycardia."

"Tachy-what?"

"It sounds complicated, but it's a condition that makes you have a fast heartbeat. Symptoms can be anxiety related."

"Oh," Bea muttered.

"It's very treatable. There are things you can do, such as avoiding caffeine and nicotine. And meditating or practicing relaxation exercises. Of course, lowering your stress level will help."

"I see."

"I also want you to make an appointment to talk to someone," Dr. Benjamin continued "Besides the tachycardia, what you experienced yesterday afternoon was most likely a panic attack. Cognitive-behavioral therapy has been shown to be very helpful in managing anxiety disorders. Do you know a professional you can make an appointment with? Or would you like a referral?"

The doctor's slow and gentle bedside manner from last night was now brisk. Bea wondered if he realized the difference.

"I received a name yesterday from the principal at my son's school," Bea said. "She recommends Dr. Martin Duffie."

"Excellent," Dr. Benjamin confirmed. "I'd like you to call him right away. I'll follow up and let him know you were under my care here. This is very important, Bea. I want you to get the help you need. You can't do this alone."

"I understand," Bea said. "I got a few things off my chest last night and I feel so much better already. I hope I can continue to improve."

"Good," the doctor said. Then he shook Bea's hand one final time and left the room, Susana doing the same and following closely behind.

The tests were easy and not at all uncomfortable, just like Dr. Benjamin had promised. When they were finished, the dayshift nurse told Bea she could get dressed and go home. They would call her with results as soon as they were ready.

26

The man behind the robotic voice was having a good morning, too. Feeling pleased with the way his initiative was progressing, he treated himself to a large plate of bacon and eggs at Lorraine's Diner. He sat in one of the booths along the wall farthest from the front door. He liked having a clear view of everyone coming and going.

To his delight, an article about his video had made the front page of the local newspaper. Several other patrons of the diner were reading it, and it gave him a thrill to see that people were paying attention.

Little did they know, he would soon begin releasing more and more detailed information until John Hughes was forced to resign from the office of mayor, and Bea Hughes was put in prison where she belonged.

He could imagine her now, her long, dark hair unstyled and pulled away from her bare face, her body swimming in an unflattering orange jumpsuit. She wouldn't look so good without her makeup and pretty clothes. He couldn't wait for her to grace the front page of the newspaper, showing the world what she really was: an unattractive, undesirable, lying *murderer*.

27

Three days later, Bea had returned to her backyard art studio to clean up the paint that had spilled the morning the anonymous call came in. Things had been relatively quiet in her life and she was buoyed by a new feeling of connection to her husband. John hadn't been home much, but when he had he was kind and attentive. She hoped things would work out for the best and that her little family of three would stay together.

Dr. Benjamin had reported good news from the medical testing and didn't think Bea had anything more serious than tachycardia and an anxiety disorder to tend to. He referred her to a cardiologist and gave her strict instructions to call him immediately if she felt pain or discomfort in her chest or a sensation like she was about to faint. She promised she would do exactly as he instructed. She felt like she had dodged a bullet. She was glad there wasn't anything more serious wrong with her heart. She called Dr. Duffie as promised and scheduled an appointment for the following week. Bea had come to terms with her medical situation. She was willing to go on medication to help with her anxiety if that's what the psychologist recommended.

No new videos had been released. As far as Bea knew, no more calls had been received either. She hoped that maybe they'd seen the end. Given the lull, John was taking the attitude that they'd wait and deal with any developments as they came up rather than taking steps to handle the situation aggressively. He reassured Bea that sometimes blackmailers got cold feet and simply went away. Deep down, Bea knew there was more to come. She avoided the newspapers and the Internet on purpose, and she enjoyed the peace and quiet with a newfound appreciation. She was more determined than ever to keep her chin up and her family under the same roof. She felt silly for having spent the night in a hotel just a few days earlier.

Max was back at school, and thanks to the administration's careful watch, Landon wasn't picking on him anymore. Max felt supported and safe. Everyone involved was happy with how things had turned out. Upon Bea's request, Lana had moved back in. Marmalade was still in Sacramento, but Natalie had promised to return him home soon. It wouldn't be long until things were back to normal. With any luck, Bea thought they'd be better than normal.

Morning sunlight streamed into Bea's art studio through the little window with the floral curtain. The light lifted Bea's spirits. Inspired, she decided she would spend the day painting whatever wanted to pour out of her. She thought of it as art therapy. She could feel herself beginning to heal after having confessed to Lana and John, and she wanted that healing to continue. She decided she'd let her husband be her inspiration today. They were planning on a romantic dinner that evening. It had been John's suggestion, offered as a way to make up for the difficulty he had put Bea through as a result of his lost temper a few days prior.

Bea reached both arms up in the air and stretched like a cat, enjoying the warm rays. Then she selected a large blank canvas and placed it on her easel. She pulled out her smartphone and selected some mood music. She chose a playlist with a selection of eighties love songs that were some of John's favorites. True Colors by Cyndi Lauper came on first. It felt like a perfect representation of their relationship. Bea could feel the music flowing through her and making her body sway along with the slow, sauntering beat. She thought about how the love she and John shared was special in its own way. Even though it wasn't what she might have imagined, it was what they had. And that was enough. John cared deeply for her. She knew that now. What kind of man would keep his wife's secret like John had if he didn't love her deeply? Bea promised herself to never take him for granted again.

She reached for a few of her favorite paintbrushes and then dipped them each in pinks, oranges, and reds. Fall would arrive soon in Northern California and the leaves would change to the very same colors as her paint. For the first time in a long time, Bea felt like she was in sync with everything around her: with her art, with the music, with the seasons, and with her husband. She began to paint a nature scene with beautiful autumn trees and two figures sitting together on a bench. The figures reminded Bea of herself and John, weathering anything that might come their way as they grew old together.

True Blue by Madonna came on next, and Bea picked up another brush then dipped it in a pastel blue the same color as the September sky. The art in front of her on the canvas took shape fast and effortlessly. It reminded Bea of her days in New York City when creating art had come easy and selling it to appreciative patrons even easier. Bea let her hands take over as one song after another played. Stroke by stroke, a masterpiece was created. When she was finished, she stepped back and assessed her work.

Fine enough for a New York City art gallery, if I do say so myself.

Filled with enthusiasm and love for her husband, Bea decided she would surprise John by giving him the painting as a gift. He had admired her artwork when they first met, and she thought perhaps this painting would provide a way for them to reconnect. She decided to call it "Fair Skies Whenever I'm With You." From the bottom of Bea's heart, she hoped it would touch John and rekindle the spark they once had. She even thought maybe they would grow close enough to make love again. Feeling amorous, Bea turned on a fan to help the paint dry, then went inside and up to the bedroom she shared with John to get ready for their special night.

As she stepped into her walk-in closet and ran her fingers along the edges of the hangers, she knew she was searching for something extra special. She wanted to wear something so pretty that it would make John weak in his knees. First, she considered a deep purple dress with a plunging neckline and a hem that fell just above the knee. John had bought it for her on a trip to Las Vegas not long after they were married. It showcased the kind of classic lines that never went out of style. But as Bea held it up against herself and looked in the mirror, it didn't seem quite right. She wanted to bring back the feelings for when they were first married, but she wanted those feelings paired with hope for a new future. She wanted something to symbolize where they were going. After rifling through other options, Bea wasn't sure she would find anything right. She considered several dresses, but ultimately decided they were either too proper or too somber for the occasion. Several others seemed too summery for September, but others yet were too wintry and covered too much skin.

Finally, Bea's fingers landed on the perfect flirty number. It was powder blue, almost the color of Cinderella's dress. It landed off the shoulder, but not too far off the shoulder, and featured cascading ruffles that fell in a lopsided line below the knee. The waistline was tailored to show off Bea's trim figure. She thought it was perfect for the evening, especially since it matched the color of the blue sky in the painting she had just created for her husband.

Bea took the dress out of the closet and tried it on, then admired herself in front of the full-length mirror. As she looked at herself, she couldn't help but remember a few days prior when she had tried on the floral print dress and thought of Travis, until Officer Tatum came to the door and caused her to hurl all over her fancy clothes.

Oh, Travis, Bea thought. *Why can I get you out of my head?*

The bright side, though, was that Bea was feeling calm and centered. No longer was she jumpy every time someone knocked on the door or the phone rang. Even though she knew intellectually that the threat remained, confessing what she'd done had worked wonders for her psyche. She only wished she had told someone sooner. Bea wasn't a Catholic, but she suspected she was beginning to understand the power of their confessional. She thought having a priest absolve her of her sins might be the best thing that could happen in her life. She made a mental note to do some research to find out what might be involved with attending mass and making a confession. Bea considered herself spiritual and not religious, but she was beginning to think it might be time for some religious guidance. Questions about forgiveness weighed heavily on her. She wanted to forgive herself. And if she ever found out who that man was, she wanted his family to forgive her for what she'd done to him.

Wishing to keep her mood upbeat, she pushed all those thoughts out of her mind. Instead, she focused on exactly how she would charm and seduce her husband. By the end of the evening, Bea intended to be making love to John in their bed, then falling asleep happily in his arms.

A few more hours remained before they were scheduled to meet, so Bea decided to put even more effort into setting the right mood. First, she changed back into her regular clothes to spruce the bedroom up without getting her dress dirty. She hung the dress on a hook in the doorway where it wouldn't be harmed while she worked. Next, she took the old sheets off the bed and replaced them with a pink satin set John used to like. In her bathroom vanity she found an old perfume that had a heavy, spicy scent that seem to turn John on, so she spritzed some on the sheets and would do the same on herself once she was dressed. The day before, Bea had picked up a big bouquet of roses at the farmer's market and so decided to put them to use. Once the bed was made neatly and turned down with the satin sheets visible, Bea plucked the petals off the roses one by one and spread them artfully around the top of bed. She and John had never made love on top of roses before, but she thought it would be a nice touch to make tonight extra special.

She had it all planned. When they arrived home, Bea would bring a bottle of wine and glasses upstairs for them to sip. The only thing missing was candlelight. Bea found a bag of tea lights in one of her vanity drawers, so she spread the tiny candles all around the bedroom. She rehearsed it in her mind. When they first arrived home she would have John wait downstairs long enough for her to scramble upstairs with the bottle of wine and light the candles. For maximum impact, Bea would change into one of her négligées that was given to her as a gift at her bridal shower. In fact, she'd wear it underneath her dress at dinner. It would be a sexy reminder of what was to come. If things went well at dinner, maybe she would guide John's hand under her skirt so he could feel the négligées for himself. Bea hoped she would turn her husband on. She hoped she still could.

When Bea had showered and done her hair, she put on the Cinderella dress, then applied makeup and jewelry to finish the look. Satisfied that the room was ready and she was as dolled up as she could get, Bea went to the living room to hang out with Max and Lana for a few minutes before heading downtown to meet John. They said they loved her dress and they showered her with compliments. When it was time to go, Bea stopped in her studio to check on the painting on her way out. It was drying nicely and would be ready to show John when they returned home. Bea thought maybe she'd make him close his eyes and wait downstairs as she got everything ready and moved the painting somewhere it could be prominently displayed. She looked forward to enjoying a good night.

As Bea pulled out of the driveway, Myra White was standing at the edge of her own yard near the road. She looked like she might wish to chat, but Bea didn't want to be late for her special evening. Bea waved at Myra and went on her way, her Cinderella dress crinkling under the seatbelt shoulder strap.

28

John had insisted they have dinner at Honey Hog, despite Bea's concerns about the scene he had made the last time they were there. He had been working to make amends for his behavior and had gone to Honey Hog twice to apologize to the owners. John assured Bea the owners were okay with it and would welcome the mayor and his wife for dinner.

Determined things would be better this time around, Bea smiled as she opened the heavy glass door at the front of the restaurant. The sun was setting, and its angle made everything sparkle. The restaurant was beautiful, inside and out. The owners had created the perfect ambience with low lighting and candles on each table. Bea hadn't remembered it being so romantic the last time she was here.

John was already seated at a table in the back. When he saw his wife walk in the front, he stood up and waved to her before the hostess could finish a greeting. Bea felt proud to be the mayor's wife. She almost felt like some kind of royalty, even if it was only in a small town. Basking in the warmth of John's affection, Bea sauntered her way around tables and chairs as she walked towards the back of the room where her husband was sitting.

"Well, don't you look pretty?" John asked as he took both of his wife's hands in his own and kissed her on the cheek.

Bea blushed. "Thank you," she said. "I wanted to look nice... For you."

"You do," John remarked as they sat down and scooted their chairs up to the table.

A young Asian waiter with an eager expression on his face arrived at the table to take their drink order. John ordered red wine for the both of them without asking Bea what she wanted, but she didn't mind. It made her feel taken care of. She liked feeling taken care of.

"I'm really glad we're doing this tonight," Bea said to her husband. "I've been thinking a lot about our future and I want you to know I'm fully committed to making things work."

John reached for Bea's hand over the top of the table and cradled it in his own. "What's gotten into you?" he asked with a smile. "You've seemed so unhappy for such a long time. In the last few days, you've been like a different person."

Bea shrugged, moving one exposed shoulder seductively. "I don't know how to explain it," she said. "Other than that I feel loved and supported by you. Maybe that's all I've needed all along. Now I'm blossoming like a flower."

"I'm glad," John said. "I really am sorry that I have

been so short with you. I guess we just got into a rut. I got into the habit of taking my frustrations out on you and that wasn't fair. In life, we all make our own choices. Even when we think we're stuck, we aren't, really. It all boils down to risks and rewards. We can do anything we want if we can stand the consequences."

"How very philosophical of you," Bea said with a laugh. "But you're right."

The conversation remained upbeat as John ordered salads for the two of them, then deviled eggs as appetizers. They were well into the main course of brisket before a negative word was spoken.

"Dammit," John said, apparently in response to someone who had walked in the front door. His brow furrowed. It was as if a dark cloud had settled over him. His mood turned sour.

"What's wrong?" Bea asked. When John didn't answer, she turned around in her chair to see for herself, only there was a large crowd gathered around the hostess stand and she couldn't make out anyone in particular who might have caused John to react the way he did. "Answer me, John. What is it?"

"Nothing for you to be concerned with," he replied gruffly.

"Come on, John," Bea said. "We were having such a nice dinner. Let's not ruin it." She turned around in her chair for a second time, but still couldn't tell who it was that was upsetting her husband. She thought about the preparations in their bedroom at home and the painting. She really wanted the night to go smoothly.

"I've got to make a trip to the restroom," John said

under his breath as he pushed himself away from the table and stood up, his brisket only partially eaten.

"Okay," Bea said, bewildered. She racked her brain but couldn't figure out what was going on. "Hurry back. I have…" He was out of sight before she could mention the surprise waiting at home. Her heart sank.

John stayed gone for what felt like an eternity. Bea's pride in her Cinderella dress turned to embarrassment as she sat alone feeling overdressed, her food getting cold while she waited on her husband to return. His absence spoke volumes about his priorities. She began to wonder if she could ever compete with his job. It seemed like she would always be a distant second. She wondered what she had been thinking referring to her dress as like Cinderella's in her own mind.

Will I always be like a helpless child in my husband's eyes, and he like an overbearing parent in mine?

When John finally returned, his face was flush and he was perspiring. His tie was ever so slightly off center.

"Sorry about that," John said. It was rare for him to apologize for anything, at least to Bea. And he had done it several times in the past week. "Gracious. Now our food is cold. You didn't have to wait on me to finish eating."

"I'm sure we can ask our waiter to have it warmed up," Bea replied. "What took you so long?" As she looked at her husband more closely, she noticed one side of his collar was turned up more than it had been when he left the table. "John, have you been in a fight?"

"What? No," he answered. "Why would you ask such a thing?"

Bea leaned forward across the table so she could talk

without other patrons overhearing. "Because your face is red and you're all sweaty." Beads of perspiration continued to form on John's brow even though he was sitting down now. "Your collar and tie are disheveled, too."

John's face turned as red as the dinner plate he was eating from. "Hush now, Beatrice. That's absurd." He began to eat the cold brisket spastically, needing something to do with his hands. A couple at a nearby table took notice. Bea could feel their eyes on her and she didn't like it.

"Where did you go?" Bea tried again.

"Out back. I had to take care of a work thing."

"What kind of a work thing?" Bea asked. "I don't mean to pry, but something strange is going on. Surely, you can see how this looks." Bea motioned in the direction of the couple who was staring at them.

John began to get frustrated with Bea's questioning. He raised a hand and moved to slap it down on the table, only he caught himself and stopped short. He leaned his head down and spoke as quietly as he could manage. "Dammit, Beatrice. Why is everything so difficult with you? Is it too much to ask that you show up, look the part, and keep your mouth shut?"

Bea recoiled, leaning all the way back in her chair. Her feelings were hurt. "I thought tonight would be different," she said. "It's looking like a replay of the last time we were here. And it's looking like I'm an idiot for believing you could change."

John sighed, still taking bites of the cold brisket, then sloshing wine around in his mouth nervously. "You're right," he said, working to calm himself down. "I do want things to be different between us. I'm under a lot of pressure at work. It's spilling into my personal life more than you know. Please forgive me. Let's try to enjoy the rest of our evening, okay?"

The waiter returned and Bea asked him to warm up their food. When he took the plates away it left John with nothing to fiddle with. He looked around, almost frantically.

"I'm serious, John," Bea prodded. "What is going on with you?"

Before John could answer, a well-dressed man with rimmed glasses and neat, jet black hair came up to the table and placed a hand on John's shoulder. The man was wearing a plaid button-down shirt, perfectly starched and tucked into his pants. Fastened to his collar was a red bowtie. He grinned as he looked down at John.

"Kyle?" John asked, surprised. "What are you…? Why…?" John was flustered. He stood up and awkwardly shook the man's hand.

"Hey, there," Kyle said as he shook John's hand, holding it a few seconds too long. He glanced at Bea, waiting for an introduction.

"Oh," John sputtered. "Where are my manners? Kyle, this is Beatrice, my... Wife."

"Pleased to meet you, Kyle," Bea said, uncertain as to what exactly was happening. She stood up to shake Kyle's hand, too.

The three of them were a strange sight. Their body language must have made the grouping look awkward to onlookers. Bea didn't want to sit down before her husband because she didn't want to be rude to Kyle. She also didn't want to be left out of whatever was taking place.

"Likewise," Kyle said, looking back at John as a prompt. Bea noticed that his movements were slow and deliberate. Something was off about him, although she couldn't tell exactly what.

"Right," John said, wiping fresh beads of perspiration from his brow. "Beatrice, this is Kyle Hodges. He works for me."

"Don't you mean *with* you?" Kyle corrected with a laugh, lowering his hand down to John's elbow and then leaning towards him as he spoke.

"Yes, with me. Sorry," John said. "I didn't mean to insinuate…"

Bea didn't think she had ever seen John like this. It made her wonder exactly how much of his work was bleeding over into his personal life. He was flustered. Discombobulated. And still sweating.

Bea and Kyle stood looking at each other for a long few minutes, sizing each other up. She wondered what role he played on John's staff, but she didn't ask. She had met a lot of John's staffers at various events over the years, but she didn't think she had ever seen Kyle before. She wondered if he was new. She wondered if he was part of the team trying to help John handle his public image after the recent negative events. If so, she thought he must have had a difficult job in front of him.

"Isn't it funny?" John asked, breaking the silence. "Kyle has worked with me for almost four years now. But I don't think the two of you have ever had occasion to meet."

Bea smiled her best fake smile at her husband. She wasn't amused. "Sure," she said.

"Better late than never," Kyle added, chuckling again. Bea couldn't tell for sure, but it sounded like his laugh would be unusual once it broke into full voice.

"Okay, then," John said, turning to Kyle. "It was good to see you. I'll walk you out."

Kyle smiled smugly, as if he had just won an important victory. His demeanor struck Bea as odd. "Fantastic, John," he said, looking at Bea while he spoke. "Beatrice, until we meet again."

Bea nodded her head and sat back down at the table as John and Kyle exited hastily through the front door of the building.

29

J ohn remained distracted for the rest of the evening.
He ate his warmed-up brisket hastily, then asked for
the check without giving Bea a chance to order
dessert.

They walked to their parked vehicles in silence, both
knowing that things weren't right between them. The past
few days had been nothing more than a good act. They
had worked hard to pretend like everything could be good,
but they both knew it shouldn't have to be this difficult.

When they arrived at the house and John pulled in the
driveway behind Bea, he rolled down his window and told
her he needed to go back into the office to handle a work
thing. He didn't even bother to step out of his SUV to
deliver the bad news. Bea hung her head, disappointed.
She looked at her art studio and thought about the
painting waiting inside.

Why did I bother?

"Can it wait until morning?" she asked hopefully,
already knowing the answer.

"Beatrice, I'm afraid it can't," John said. "I'm sorry."

There was again. An apology. John was out of sorts, that was for sure. He was not a man who had ever spent much time apologizing.

Without saying another word, Bea got out of her van and closed the door. She didn't mention the rose petals on the bed upstairs, or the wine chilling in the refrigerator, or the painting she had so lovingly created for her husband as a gesture of her desire for a fresh start. John sped out of the driveway without looking back. His priorities were elsewhere. It seemed to Bea as if her husband had hardly given her a second thought.

How disrespectful and frustrating. Travis wouldn't have treated me like this.

The evening was nice and Bea had a lot on her mind, so she stayed outside in the backyard under the string lights for a while before going in. She knew Max would be in bed already, and Lana would probably doze off in front of the TV. Bea knew a conversation with her best friend Gabby was long overdue, so she called her and invited her over for a drink on the patio. Gabby lived close by and was glad to receive Bea's invite. It took her less than fifteen minutes to show up, a box of decadent chocolate-covered strawberries in hand.

"Bea, my friend," Gabby said as she reached up to hug Bea's neck. "You're all dressed up tonight. Tell me. Where have you been?"

Gabrielle was from Jamaica and had the most charming accent Bea had ever heard. She had broad, round features and pretty brown skin. She was in her early forties, but looked decades younger. Gabby was elegant in a way Bea sometimes wished she could emulate. Gabby was always dressed fashionably and wore the perfect outfit for every occasion. Bea still had her blue Cinderella dress on, and even though Gabby had no idea what her friend was wearing, she showed up in a dress of her own that was nearly as nice. Gabby's interest in fashion wasn't solely for pleasure. She owned a jewelry store downtown and had to dress nicely for business.

"Oh," Bea began, feeling relaxed in the presence of her best friend. "I've had quite a night. Quite a week, for that matter. I've just come from dinner at Honey Hog with my public-figure husband. You know how that goes. I wanted a private dinner where we could reconnect and have some quality time together, but all I got was prying eyes, a random colleague of John's showing up, and my husband's short temper."

"Sounds about right," Gabby said with a laugh. Bea was so glad to see her. She hadn't seen her friend for more than a week, not since before the phone call that had rocked her semi-peaceful world. When Gabby had dropped Max off back at home, Bea hadn't been there to greet her.

"I've missed you," Bea said. "I know I should have called. It's been crazy."

"No need to explain, lady."

"How is it that we live so close to each other, but we don't get together near enough?" Bea asked.

"I'm available," Gabby said. "I'm not the one with the famous husband who drags me out for show." Gabby laughed as she said it, but she knew as well as Bea did that it was no laughing matter. Not really. "So fill me in on what's happening. Max told me some stories. It seemed like there was much more below the surface. What he told me was probably the tip of the iceberg, no?"

"Yep, you've got it," Bea replied. "I'll tell you everything, but first I need some of those chocolate-covered strawberries you brought to bribe me with. I need to be well fed if I'm expected to tell my story again. It's long. And complicated."

The friends poured themselves glasses of wine then ate chocolate-covered strawberries in silence as they looked up at the stars together. Bea knew she could tell Gabby anything. She wished she had told her about the night at Eagle's Point a long time ago. Gabby knew about Travis, but she hadn't been privy to the reason that Bea had broken things off with him. Gabby also knew how John was. It was no secret that she wished Bea would leave him. Gabby wasn't the type to tell her friend what to do though. She was strong, confident, and had a good head on her shoulders, but she wanted Bea to come to things in her own time and her own way. Gabby would never try to force the issue. She was more of a quiet encourager for her friend. A cheerleader who was always in Bea's corner.

When Bea was ready, she told Gabby the entire story, sparing no detail. She explained what had happened over the course of the past week and then she filled in the blanks by explaining what had happened during the incident a decade ago. Gabby's eyes grew wide as she listened, but her face showed no sign of doubting her friend's character. Just like Lana and Travis had done, Gabby made it clear she was on Bea's side and would stand by her.

"What did I do to deserve a best friend like you?" Bea asked as she leaned her head on her friend's shoulder. "I'm touched that you will stand by me after everything you've just heard."

"Of course, I will," Gabby said. "Don't give it a second thought. That's what friends are for. And besides, I think that man at Eagle's Point got what he deserved. I know I don't have a child of my own, but if I did, I'd like to think I would have done the same as you. Only I probably would have hit that man a few more times with the bat and kicked him around a bit before pushing him over the edge. He deserved to suffer."

Bea felt a pang of guilt at Gabby's flippant attitude. "I don't know, Gab," she said. "I took a man's life. He was a human being. He probably had a family who waited for him to come home. That's terrible, and I'm responsible."

"I can't say that I agree," Gabby replied. "That man had your child and was taking him away, after having altered his appearance, no less. That's sick. The kind of sick that doesn't deserve to live. If he had survived to stand trial, I guarantee you he would have been put away for the rest of his life. Or better yet, sent to the electric chair."

"I never thought about it that way," Bea said.

"Then think about it that way now," Gabby persisted. "Do you know what they do to child molesters in prison?"

"No, I don't," Bea replied. "I'm not real familiar with prison life other than what I've seen on *Orange is the New Black*."

Gabby shook her head from side to side slowly with a smile on her face. She had always seemed somehow savvier than Bea. She was more worldly, being from Jamaica and having traveled abroad. She was also smarter, Bea wasn't ashamed to admit. Having a smart friend like Gabby often came in handy. Whenever there was a dilemma that Bea couldn't figure out on her own, she could always count on Gabby to brainstorm and come up with a solution. She really should have told Gabby about her predicament a long time ago.

"What?" Bea asked teasingly. "I didn't want to google prison life and make myself look guilty."

"Bea Hughes, you never cease to amaze me."

"I'll take that as a compliment."

"But in all seriousness," Gabby continued. "Even hardened criminals have no sympathy for child molesters. In the prison, guards will look the other way while the other prisoners serve up what's coming to them. If you ask me, you did the world a favor by taking that guy out."

Bea raised one heel off the ground and turned her toes around on the brick patio as she thought about what Gabby had said. "But what about his family, Gab? He must have had one. If not a partner and a family of his own, at least a mother? A father? Everyone is somebody's baby."

"You need to stop thinking about it like that," Gabby insisted. "That man tried to take *your* baby. Do you even know what he did to Max when he had him in the bathroom? I mean, it sounds like he had the time and might have molested our boy. Max was probably too young to have known what to report, but that mess has lasting effects on a person's mental health."

"No, I don't know what happened in the bathroom.

That very question has haunted my nightmares. Well, that along with the prospect of being taken away from my family and arrested. Gabby, I've lived in fear every day for ten years. It has changed me."

"Yeah, I get that," Gabby affirmed. "And I've noticed the difference in you. Looking back, it all makes sense now. I thought it was about John. It seemed like your self-esteem took a hit when you got with him. And hell, Bea, I thought Travis was a good thing. You didn't ask my opinion when you broke it off with him, but if you had, I would have told you I thought you were making a mistake It seemed like you were depriving yourself of a good man who could love you right because you didn't feel you were worthy of that love. As your friend, that makes me sad."

"It makes me sad, too. More than you know."

Gabby sat up straight and put both hands on her thighs like she was formulating a plan. She stared out at Bea's art studio across the lawn. Bea could almost see the wheels turning in her mind.

"It's time to reframe this," Gabby announced. "Now that I know the whole story, I see it all differently. For starters, you need to dig deep and get in touch with your old self. We need the old Bea Denton who believed in herself and sold her paintings in New York City galleries to make a comeback. John Hughes can only hold you back if you let him. And the same goes for what happened at Eagle's Point."

"Prison can hold me back."

"Hush," Gabby said. "None of that talk. There's hope for you, Bea."

"Do you really think so?"

"I know so. You can either feel guilty that a man died and blame yourself, or you can feel proud that you defended your son against certain evil. Not to mention, you rid the world of that evil and probably saved other kids from being his victims. Many people would call you a hero."

The word made Bea shudder. She didn't feel like a hero. "I don't know about that."

Gabby pursed her lips as she continued to think. Bea waited patiently, thrilled that someone was helping her take this on. Lana and Travis were compassionate listeners who would support Bea, but Gabby was a go-getter who would offer more. Bea was happy to take any help she could get. Some kind-hearted prodding from her friend seemed like exactly what Bea needed right now.

"Let's do this," Gabby began. "Let's start with a little Internet research. I'll do it on my computer if you're worried about using one of your own, But we need to find out who this guy was. Do you know if his body was ever recovered?"

"No," Bea said. "I don't. I've been sort of like an ostrich with my head in the sand about the whole thing. I've tried to focus on Max and to be grateful for every day I get to spend with him."

"That's understandable," Gabby said. "But it won't help you put this drama to rest, which is what needs to happen. I want you to start thinking about taking back control of your life instead of just waiting to be tossed around like a leaf in the wind."

That description resonated with Bea. "Wow," she said.

"That's exactly how I feel. Like a leaf in the wind. Light and powerless against its forces."

"Will you let me help?" Gabby asked. "I sure would like to do whatever I can."

"Yes," Bea replied adamantly. "I need all the help I can get. I know with you, I'll be in capable hands. Let's do it!"

"Good!" Gabby echoed.

"But what about my situation with John and the impact the hooded figure on video is having on his career?" Bea asked. "I don't want to get too focused on the man from Eagle's Point and lose sight of the damage that's happening right here in the present day. For better or worse, anything that happens with me is tied to John, and it could make or break the career he's worked so hard for."

"The way I see it," Gabby clarified. "We have two separate issues here. That means we have two tasks at hand."

"Okay."

"The first is to find out everything we can about the man you saved Max from. If he was as bad of a guy as you think, we might get some answers that could help ease your guilty conscience."

"That would be amazing," Bea said. "I hadn't thought such a turn of events would be possible."

"Yeah, well, I know it's a long shot, but if he had hurt other kids in the past, you might even be able to come forward and be hailed a hero."

Bea put one hand on her forehead as she tried to

imagine that scenario. It seemed too good to be true. "And the second issue?"

"That would be the matter of John Hughes. I'd like to see you getting the love you deserve. I don't know what the answers are... With John. Or with Travis. But you're my best friend, Bea. I want to see you happier."

"Would you believe that John thinks Travis is the man on the video?"

"And what do you think?" Gabby asked.

Bea didn't hesitate before replying. "I guess Travis has a motive, like John said. Because he seems to really want to get back with me. He's been blowing up my phone with calls and texts since I saw him a few days ago."

"Why haven't you answered him?"

"I contacted Travis because I wanted to warn him about the anonymous caller who said they knew what I'd done. I felt like he had a right to know since he was there that night and could end up tangled up in this. But I've been trying to make a fresh start with John. To make things work between us again. I just want to keep my family together, you know?"

"I hear you. Do you think you're making the right decision?" Gabby continued.

Bea chuckled. "What are you? A shrink? You're answering every question with a question."

"And how does that make you feel?" Gabby said in her most therapist-like voice. The ladies laughed together.

"That reminds me," Bea added. "Jenny Maguire, the principal at Max's school, gave me the name of a psychologist she thinks I should go see. And the attending physician at the hospital the other day recommended I follow her advice. I haven't called the guy yet."

"Let's get busy crossing some important things off your to-do list, shall we? Give me a day or so and I'll see what I can come up with. Watch for my call. I'll soon have news of progress. Okay, friend?"

Gratefully, Bea agreed. With Gabby's guidance, the two of them would take action towards sorting out Bea's jumbled up life.

30

B y the time Bea's head hit the pillow, her confidence had been bolstered by her discussion with Gabby. The disappointment she had felt a few hours earlier about John not appreciating her efforts had begun to fade and she was more hopeful. Even though Gabby had never been married and didn't have a child of her own, Bea valued her opinion. Bea had always assumed Gabby didn't marry because owning the jewelry store kept her so busy. But maybe it also had something to do with the fact that Gabby refused to settle. Bea thought she would do well to follow her friend's example.

As she drifted off to sleep, Bea let herself imagine a world where she told the police what she had done and they didn't arrest her. Gabby was right. That man had been trying to take her baby. Maybe it was the wine affecting her, but the thought seemed almost too good to be true.

Could what I did be considered self-defense? Would that clear me in the eyes of the law?

To ease her mind, Bea worked to picture herself as an honest woman, free and clear. She imagined herself being right by Max's side during all of those special days she had written letters for. Wouldn't it be grand if she could deliver those letters in person? Bea fell into dreamland, content.

When her alarm sounded the next morning, Bea was surprised to find that John was not in bed next to her. The covers on his side were still pulled taut. He hadn't come home at all last night. Bea felt sad as she thought about the implications. No matter how distant her husband had been in times past, he had always come home at night. Seeing him there on the other side of the bed when Bea opened her eyes every morning had been a comfort. His absence made her feel adrift. Like Gabby had so eloquently said, a leaf in the wind.

Bea got up and got herself dressed for the day, then went downstairs to make breakfast and eat with Max and Lana. She expected a quiet morning, but those hopes were dashed when Max walked into the room and she saw the look of concern on his face.

"What's wrong?" Bea asked Max as she gave him a hug. "You look like something has upset you."

"You probably don't want to know," Max replied sheepishly.

"Nonsense. If something has upset you, then I most definitely want to know. You're my boy. We're a team, remember?"

Max shrugged his shoulders as he looked up at his mom. "It's another video," he said. "It was posted online early this morning, and it's already had a bunch of views."

"It's… Worse than the last," Lana added, the worry evident on her face.

"That bad?" Bea asked as she walked over to give her mom a hug. She was trying to make light of it for Max's benefit, although she knew he'd probably have to face more blowback in school. What a mess.

"See for yourself," Max said, thrusting his smartphone towards his mom's face. "It's loaded up. Just hit play."

Bea did as instructed. As the picture moved, she recognized the same hooded figure, which spoke in the same robotic voice. It made her shudder. She was growing angry at whoever was doing this. Why were they so bent on exposing her, anyway? What did they stand to gain?

"Keep watching," Max said when Bea's eyes drifted away from the screen. "You're not paying close enough attention, Mom." He used his finger to rewind the video, starting it at the beginning.

"Okay, okay," she said. "I'm watching."

Tuned into the message this time, Bea listened closely as the hooded figure repeated his claim. Rosemary Run Mayor John Hughes was covering up a murder that his wife committed. Only this time, the hooded figure's claim was followed by footage of Bea being wheeled out of the high school and loaded up into the ambulance. Whoever shot this footage couldn't have been more than ten feet away.

As the hooded figure spoke, the words appeared on the screen for emphasis. The format was the same as last time. It seemed like the same person, that was for sure.

"Beatrice Hughes is a cold-blooded murderer. She murdered a man at Eagle's Point. John Hughes knew about it and didn't notify the authorities. May they burn in hell for what they've done."

The video ended with a fiery scene and a demonic laugh in the background.

The day the anonymous call had come in on the landline and Bea answered, fear had prevailed. But today, after watching the latest video, Bea was furious. "Damn," she said. "What does this person want from me?"

Lana shot Bea a look that told her to tread lightly. Max was around and hanging on his mother's every word.

"Is it true?" Max asked. It was a reasonable question, but one Bea had not been prepared for. "I remember us going to Eagle's Point when I was little. I used to play on the playground there."

Bea looked at her mom for guidance. She was tempted to tell Max the truth right then and there. She certainly didn't want to lie to him, but it was a lot to place on his young shoulders. Bea knew she needed to think carefully before involving him.

Before she could answer her son, there was a loud knock at the front door.

"I wonder who that could be," Bea mumbled. "It's not even seven AM."

"I'll get it!" Max offered, moving towards the door.

Bea was cautious about what her son might be stepping into, so she told him to wait while she answered it herself. "I've got it," she said. She had a feeling it wasn't good news.

Before Bea opened the front door, she stepped close to it and looked through the peephole. The light was still dim outside and visibility was low. She flipped the switch to turn the porch light on. As she did, she saw a sudden burst of light pointing back towards the door. Unsure of what was happening and against her better judgment, she opened the front door.

The moment the morning air hit her skin, camera flashes blinked all around her. A man dressed in a business suit and tie was shoving a microphone into her face while several others crowded behind him trying to do the same.

"Mrs. Hughes!" the man shouted, assaulting Bea's senses. "Is it true that you committed a murder at Eagle's Point, like the video claims?"

Before Bea could process what was happening, much less answer, the other microphones were coming at her and questions were being shouted from the crowd. She couldn't tell who was saying what. It was all a dizzying blur.

"Is your husband aware of the crime you committed?" a lady in a blue pants suit asked forcefully.

"Are you going to turn yourself in now that you've been exposed?" a second lady in a pink fitted dress shouted.

"Have you been contacted by the police?" the man in the front tried.

"Mrs. Hughes! Mrs. Hughes!"

They were like a pack of rabid animals, pushing and shoving to get close to Bea and have their questions heard. She had seen this type of thing in the movies, but never in real life. She hadn't experienced anything like it herself.

"Mrs. Hughes, is your husband home? Why isn't his vehicle in the driveway? Have the two of you split up because of the mounting accusations against you?" Now it was getting personal.

Bea felt a shoulder brush against hers. *Max*. He had stepped into the door frame and joined her in view of the cameras. His mouth hung open as he looked at the gaggle of reporters and cameramen on his front lawn.

"Mom, what are they doing here?" he whispered, the morning light shining on his troubled face.

Cameras clicked even more furiously, and the flashes came faster as the media zoomed in on Max. The assault snapped Bea back to reality and out of her daze. "No comment," she said matter-of-factly to the reporters, then she closed the front door and locked it tight, letting out an audible sigh of relief.

"I'm so sorry about that, Max," she said, knowing full well that this was just the beginning. "Those reporters are jackals. They prey on other people's difficulties. Try not to pay them any attention."

"It's a shameful profession, really," Lana added, wrinkling up her mouth as she stepped to the window and looked out at them.

Max watched his mom like a hawk. He looked determined to get answers. "Was what they said about Dad true? That that the two of you have separated? Why isn't he home? He doesn't usually leave for work this early." The speed of his words went faster and faster, and they became higher pitched.

Bea was at a loss. She had no idea what to do, yet she knew she needed to do something decisive to reassure her son. Lana could see her daughter's discomfort, but wasn't in much of a position to help. Bea was Max's mother. As his grandmother, Lana knew she needed to let her take the lead.

Before Bea could explain, they heard a commotion out front. The three of them walked to the window closest to the driveway and peaked out around the shades to see what was going on. Bea, Max, and Lana huddled together as they tried to glimpse what was happening without exposing too much of themselves in the window. Being in close physical proximity to her mother and son helped steady Bea. An image flashed through her mind of the three of them being like the center of the wheel, standing back to back with everything else in the world at arm's length spinning around them. She thought that as long as the three of them had each other, they could face anything.

"It's Dad!"

The familiar sounds of John's SUV coming to a stop and then cutting its engine made their way inside. No wonder his arrival had captured the media's attention. They began to shout questions at John even louder than they had at Bea. It sounded like a feeding frenzy in the wild. Even though Bea was mad at John and wasn't sure how they could move forward together, she felt bad that he was under attack.

As the noise of the shouting reached a fever pitch, John unlocked the back door with his key and then burst inside, tightening the shades down behind him. "My God! These people are ruthless," he said as he began to pace around the kitchen while Bea, Max, and Lana looked on. He was wearing the same clothes he'd had on at Honey Hog last night and he looked like he hadn't showered.

"Dad, where have you been?" Max asked eagerly. "Did you stay out all night?"

John eyeballed Bea, apparently wondering what she had told their son. "Don't look at me," Bea said. "I'd like to know the answer to Max's questions, too."

John hesitated. He chewed his fingernails as he continued to pace. It was an unusual thing for him to do. Bea didn't think she'd ever seen him bite his fingernails in all the time she'd known him.

Lana made the best offer she could. "Bea, dear," Lana began. "How about Max and I finish breakfast while you and John go upstairs to talk? I could make my homemade cinnamon rolls everybody loves. It won't take long to whip them up. I know how Max likes them. It will be a special treat."

"That would be lovely, Mom," Bea said, not taking her eyes off her husband. "We have some catching up to do."

Max seemed interested in the cinnamon rolls, but not totally convinced. "What about school?" he asked. "If we don't leave soon, we won't make it on time."

"School isn't our top priority right now! Will you give it a rest?" John roared, lashing out at his son. Max took a step back as if he'd been pushed by John's rage. He wasn't accustomed to being talked to this way.

Lana put her arm around Max. "I've got him," she said softly. "Go. Talk."

Annoyed, John stomped upstairs. Bea followed.

31

The bedroom door slammed hard in Bea's face. John was on a tear, perhaps worse than ever before. But Bea wouldn't be deterred. She needed to talk to her husband and come to some shared understanding. She opened the door and entered the bedroom. When she did, she saw John standing near the rose petals she had placed in a bowl on top of a dresser.

"Did Travis give you these?" he shouted. He looked rabid, like a junkyard dog. The old John she once knew seemed a million miles away. "Have you forgotten that Travis is the reason we're in this mess?"

"No," Bea said emphatically. "Why would you think they're from him?"

"Gee, I don't know," John barked. "Do I really have to spell it out for you? I'm not stupid, you know."

"John, he's not behind the videos. Travis wouldn't do something like this."

"Well, he's my number one suspect," John said. "I'm damn near certain it's him. If it isn't Travis appearing on video, then he's behind it. Maybe he's hired somebody to stand in.''

"*Stop it.* The rose petals were for you... For us," Bea explained. "I had a romantic evening planned. I spread them out on the bed. Last night..."

John raised his eyebrows as he made the connection. "Oh," he said. But it didn't stop his tirade. "Well, whatever."

Bea closed the door behind her and locked it so they wouldn't be disturbed. She pulled the chair out from her makeup table and sat down, careful that her body language wasn't threatening. She didn't want to pick a fight. John was doing enough of that for the both of them.

"What do you want from me?" John asked.

Bea thought it was a strange question. "What do I want from you?" Bea echoed. "I want you to be a good husband and father. To care for me and Max, and to treat us nicely. What do you think I want from you?"

John began to pace again, agitated. "You're never happy," he said.

"That's not true," Bea said. "I was happy yesterday. I was looking forward to our special night together."

"Yeah, well, I can't control what happened," John said, dismissing her. "There are things you don't understand."

Bea took a breath. "You used those same words the other day in the hospital. What is it I don't understand? Enlighten me."

"You wouldn't understand even if I told you!" he raged, still pacing.

"Come on, John," Bea pleaded. "Try me. After our talk the other night where we cleared the air, I thought we were in this together. I *want* us to be in this together. There are reporters on our lawn, for God's sake. It seems like we ought to be in this together."

John stepped towards the window and peeked around the shade.

"Are they still out there?" Bea asked.

"Yes."

Bea twirled a few strands of her silky hair as she thought about how to bridge the chasm that had developed between them. She didn't know what to say or what to do that would bring them back together like they once were.

"John," she began, as calmly as she could manage. "I made you a painting yesterday. I spent all day working on it."

He paused and looked at her, tilting his head toward one shoulder. "That's... It's nice of you, Beatrice. It really is."

"Do you want to know what I painted?"

"Sure," John said, stepping away from the window and sitting down on the side of the bed.

"It's an old couple sitting beside each other on a bench, in the fall. It's you and me. It's the future I want for us. I want us to weather life's storms together."

John's demeanor softened. He shook his head and raised his hands out in front of him. He was at a loss for words.

"Have I really changed that much?" Bea asked.

"What? No, it's got nothing to do with that."

Bea was quiet as she mustered the nerve to ask him the question she most wanted an answer to. "John, where were you last night? And tell me the truth. I deserve that much."

"I already told you," he sniped. "I had to deal with a work thing. It… It took all night."

A single tear fell down Bea's cheek. She wiped it away quickly, embarrassed. She wanted to be strong. She wanted to hold it together.

"John," she began again. "Is there another woman?"

Her question was innocent enough, but it sent John into an even wilder rage.

"Goddamnit, Beatrice!" he yelled at the top of his lungs. Max and Lana could surely hear now. "Would you get off my back? There's no other woman! How many times do I have to tell you that before you get it through your thick skull?" John panted, leaping off the bed and heaving his body around the room as if it were a truck he was driving instead of a part of him. "Leave me the fuck alone, for Christ's sake! You're a dead weight around my neck that I just can't seem to shake. Or a prison sentence I'm destined to serve. I can't even breathe you're so far up my ass."

John began batting at things around the room. He knocked down picture frames. Then he slammed his fist on a nightstand as a stack of books went flying. He pivoted quickly, succumbing to a full-blown tantrum now. He kicked the side of the bed. And in one dramatic movement, he picked up a lamp and tore it from the wall, then sent it hurtling across the room. It landed near Bea's legs, a sharp corner hitting the side of her knee on its way down.

John had never been violent before. He had been

short-tempered, critical, and condescending. True. But it had never escalated to violence. The night he flipped the table at Honey Hog was the first time Bea had ever seen him get physical. As he destroyed their bedroom in a blind rage, the situation became crystal clear to her. No one had been hurt when he flipped the table. But she knew that someone would if she allowed this to continue. John was so wrapped up in his own anger that he hadn't even realized the lamp hit Bea's leg. As she sat watching his destruction, she realized that even though he hadn't thrown the lamp at her on purpose, one day he would. It was a perfect parallel to the status of their lives. Whether or not John intended it, the damage to Bea was increasing.

In that moment, Bea realized their relationship would not get better. No second chance would change things. No painting or romantic dinner would make it right. Their marriage was over.

32

T he man behind the robotic voice was growing ever more pleased with himself. He hadn't thought things would go so smoothly. His plan was proceeding even better than he had imagined.

The pressure on John and Bea Hughes was mounting. Now that he had revealed the location where the murder took place, reporters could dig for details and come to their own conclusions. The media was on it like a dog with a bone. The damage to the Hughes' reputation was worsening. And John was cracking like a nut under the pressure. If they weren't ruined already, it wouldn't take much longer. Their time was running out.

33

"Hey, it's me," Bea said when he answered the phone.
"Babe! I've been so worried about you."

"Can we meet?"

"Right now?" Travis asked with a laugh. "You don't respond to me for days, and then you expect me to show up on demand when you do?" He was teasing already. What a relief.

"That's right," Bea said, joking as well. "Do you have a problem with that, Mr. Earl?"

"I definitely do not. For you, I'll drop everything and be on my way. Our usual spot?"

"See you there."

34

I t wasn't easy to get out of the house.

    Max was content enough to skip school for the day and stay home with his grandmother. They all agreed that was best. Bea was no longer concerned with what John did. She didn't believe he would physically hurt his son, so she didn't think twice about leaving Max at home while John was there. At least not for a little while. Lana would keep Max in another part of the house to avoid John's foul mood. But evading those jackal reporters took effort.

They swarmed around Bea as she made her way to her van, filming her every move and shouting questions at her while shoving microphones in her face. She'd had the forethought to wear a baggy sweater, and she used the ample room inside to use the garment as a shield for her face. When she got in her van and drove out the driveway, reporters and camera crew threw themselves in front of her path. It was almost as if they wanted her to hit them. It took a solid ten minutes for Bea to make her way onto the road and out of the crosshairs.

Not wanting to be recognized, she drove to Gabby's. Her friend hadn't left for work yet, so they could switch vehicles in the garage without anyone noticing. Finally, free and with her pulse pounding, Bea got in Gabby's car and sped out of town towards the bay. It was a beautiful day, the kind with just the right amount of sunshine and a light, comfortable breeze.

As she drove, Bea laughed out loud at the absurdity of what was happening in her life. She still wasn't sure how things had gone so wrong, but she was beginning to understand that maybe they had needed to go wrong so that somehow, someday they could go right. Maybe things had to fall apart for the pieces of her life to be reassembled and put back together.

She owed Travis an apology. And she owed him an explanation. He had proven himself, and he deserved to know the whole truth.

When she arrived at their old meeting place, Galley Books, Bea parked on a side street and walked the half a block to the front of the building. She and Travis had spent countless hours there, canoodling at corner tables while thumbing through books and sipping bubbly beverages from the store's old-fashioned soda fountain. Even though Bea hadn't been to Galley in a long time, the place looked and felt the same. Monty, the owner's toy poodle, greeted her with a sniff as she walked in the door. He had been just a pup when she'd seen him last.

"Monty!" Bea gushed as she stooped down and stroked his curly gray fur. "Look at you, old pal." It took the dog a minute, but he seemed to recognize her. It felt good to be in one of her old favorite places, independent of John and enjoying her day.

Bea was still scratching Monty's chin when Travis' familiar voice reached her ears. He had been sitting at their usual table, but got up when he saw her walk in. "Bea, babe," he said as he helped her stand up. "It's so good to see you again. I've been so worried. Are you okay? Your health, I mean?"

"Hey! Yes, nothing serious," she said.

"Good. Then you won't mind if I do this." Travis advanced, wrapped one arm around Bea's waist, pulling her tightly to him. He put his warm lips on hers and kissed her slowly and deeply. For a split second, Bea started to pull away, but thought better of it. She let herself melt into him, succumbing to the urge that she had suppressed for so long. Being with Travis like this, kissing him in public, made her feel alive.

"My, my, sir! What a welcome," Bea teased when their lips finally parted.

"Was it too much?" Travis asked.

"Maybe," she replied. "But no, not really. I'm not ashamed to admit that I've pictured that kind of welcome on more than one occasion."

"Does that mean…?" Travis began. "Wait. If you're calling me, meeting me at our old spot, and kissing me… And, oh my God, Bea! You took your wedding ring off."

Bea laughed and smiled as her cheeks turned pink with excitement. "Let's just say we have a lot to talk about."

They walked hand-in-hand back to their usual table.

Travis had taken the liberty of ordering them both sodas from the fountain. He had ordered cherry for Bea.

"You remembered," she remarked. "How sweet."

"Of course, I did."

They sat down and sipped their sodas, but couldn't keep their hands off each other. Bea could tell Travis was holding back, not wanting to be presumptuous. But she had already made up her mind. She was ready.

Bea slid one hand under the table and placed it on the inside of Travis' thigh. He sat up straight in response, puffing his chest out and smiling. Slowly, she let her fingers brush upward towards his most sensitive spot as she watched him squirm. No one else was sitting close to them, so she had some fun with it. She moved her whole body close to Travis and nuzzled into his neck, dragging her bottom lip to his earlobe. His masculine scent made her wild with desire.

"I want you, Travis Earl," she whispered into his ear. "I want you to take me back to your loft, then peel off all of my clothes and make sweet, sweet love to me."

"Bea," Travis said, his voice cracking as he tried to maintain his composure. "Are you sure? You have a lot going on. I don't want to complicate things. When I make love to you again, I want you to be sure."

Using her free hand, Bea grabbed Travis' shoulder, hoisting herself onto his lap and straddling him in his chair. She didn't care that there were other people in the bookstore. The only thing on her mind was reuniting her body with Travis'. She placed her lips just inches from his as she looked deeply into his eyes. "I'm sure."

Convinced, Travis stood up, holding onto Bea as her

legs remained wrapped around his waist. Bea could feel him throbbing beneath her as her body came alive. Every touch, every smell, and every movement sent shivers up and down her spine. It was all they could do to restrain themselves as they walked the three blocks west to Travis' loft. Bea had half a notion to step into an alley or behind a building and lift her skirt as she pressed into Travis. If they had been caught, she didn't think she would have cared. She wanted him desperately.

When they got to his place and climbed the stairs in the back, they kissed and grabbed at each other as they stumbled inside. The door had barely closed behind them before they were naked, items of clothing thrown around haphazardly in their hurry to get them off. They didn't even make it to the bed. Travis hoisted Bea onto a kitchen counter, where they became blessedly intertwined. Within minutes, their sexual tension was released in the most pleasant way.

Bea felt alive. Like her old self again.

Now that's what I'm talking about.

35

"Ooh-wee," Travis exclaimed as he tilted his head back, an expression of pure joy on his face. "I've been waiting for this for, well, forever. At least, it feels that way."

Bea smiled bigger than she had for as long as she could remember. She often smiled big with Max, of course. But this was different. "Travis Earl, I think you just rocked my world."

"Good! So, you're saying my performance was up to snuff?"

"Oh yes," Bea said. "High marks, for sure." She leaned her head down on Travis' shoulder, running her fingers over one chiseled bicep.

"Bea, babe?"

"Yes?"

"I hope you know my feelings for you are about far more than just the physical. Don't get me wrong. The physical is like the biggest firework show at the biggest Fourth of July celebration," Travis said with a laugh. "But

I care about you... Who you are deep down. It doesn't matter what you're going through or what you've done. I see you. And I *choose* you."

"I know you do," Bea said softly.

"Bea, I love you."

Travis had never said that before. Even though Bea knew it, it meant something else for her to hear the words. "Travis, it might not have always seemed like it, but I love you, too. I always have."

Travis leaned his forehead against Bea's and gazed into her eyes. "I wasn't kidding when I said I want a real future with you. A happily ever after. I want to put a ring on your finger that they won't take off until your last day here on Earth. If it's what you want."

"I think I do," Bea said. "I need a little time to sort myself out and get a solid foundation under me and Max, but I want you in my life... From now on."

"I want you to be sure," Travis said. "I won't be a consolation prize. If you have any doubt, I'll wait. Hell, I've waited this long. What's a while longer? Wait. Don't answer that."

They both laughed together.

"I'm leaving John," Bea said. "At least that's settled."

"Finally!" Travis said. "What made you decide?"

"I'm not completely sure. But the pressure we've been under lately seems to have put a microscope on our relationship. It has shaken me up and made me take an honest look at how things are. I've lived in fear for a long time, afraid to make a change. Now that change is coming whether I like it or not, I've gained a new-found freedom to make my life my own."

"I can see that."

"I think John's a good guy, fundamentally," Bea continued. "He loves his son, that's for sure. And he has been good to me in several important ways. But I don't think our marriage is what a marriage is supposed to be. I can't put my finger on it, but something big is missing. It has been since the beginning. I think I mistook John's caring for me as what a spouse is supposed to be, when his affection is more paternal, you know? I guess I've finally come around to believe that I deserve more. And really, John deserves more, too. I'm not sure what would make him happy. But it isn't me. It's time for both of us to move on."

"I know it's been hard on you," Travis said. "I'm sorry about that. But since the day I met you, I knew that you and I belonged together. When you walked into my furniture store and I saw your face, something settled over me. And *I knew*."

"Really?" Bea asked. "You've never told me that before."

"I didn't want to lean on you too hard," Travis explained. "You know the whole thing... About how if you love something, you should set it free. I wanted you to come back to me. To choose me. When we commit to each other, I want it to be for good."

Bea thought this was the most serious conversation she'd ever had about her life. She and John had never talked like this. In all their years of marriage, John had never said he thought they belonged together. His marriage proposal had always felt more like a business transaction. An acquisition, even.

"I want that too," Bea said. "I've never had it." She continued to lean on Travis as she ran her fingers gently over his muscular arms. A clock above his refrigerator ticked softly. It reminded her of the one in her art studio. "Hey," she added. "Jenny Maguire gave me the name of a psychologist she recommends I see, and I think it's a good idea. I have a lot to unpack so I can understand why I've made the decisions I did. I want to do better."

"Babe, that's great," Travis said. "I support you completely."

"Will you go with me?"

"Like drive you there and sit in the waiting room? Or come inside?"

Bea chuckled. "I guess that's a fair question since I left you in the car when I went into the conference at Max's school the other day. But yes, I mean for you to come in with me. *Be* in counseling with me. So we can start the next phase of our relationship off right."

Travis smiled. "Yes, absolutely," he said, beaming. "In case you haven't noticed, I'm pretty agreeable. And beyond that, I'd do anything for you, Bea. You could ask me to scale the face of Mount Everest and I'd gear right up and go do it. You are my everything. I'm just happy for the chance to show you how much you mean to me."

"I might have an anxiety disorder," Bea said.

"Yeah, I got that idea at the school the other day. But you don't see me backing off. I'm here to stay."

"I might also have a minor heart condition."

"Whoa, what?" Travis asked. "I wasn't expecting that. Is it okay? Are *you* okay?"

"Emphasis on minor," Bea clarified. "But I have to go see a cardiologist. Something about a fast heartbeat."

"Alright, that sounds manageable. What else have you got?"

Bea shook her head as she thought about the enormity of it. "You know, the teensy problem of what I've done and the person who knows about it. The person releasing videos with information designed to expose me. Oh, plus, John having covered it up."

"Ah, that little thing." Travis said as he settled in while Bea told him the rest of the story.

36

By the time Bea and Travis left his loft together to get some lunch, she had made another big decision. What Gabby had said about being tossed around like a leaf in the wind had made an impression on her. Bea didn't want to live that way. She didn't want to live in fear, cowering every time someone knocked on the door or the telephone rang. It was time she reframe her situation, just like Gabby had pointed out. It was time she took control of everything in her power. At least, this way, she could sleep at night knowing she had done everything she could. At least, this way, Max would know his mother was fallible, but also honest and good.

"I'm going to confess," Bea proclaimed after placing her sandwich order at Lorraine's Diner. A perky young waitress named Kai brought the happy couple two glasses of cold tea.

"Babe," Travis said once Kai was out of earshot. "That's heavy."

"The only way out of this is through it," Bea said.

"Are you going to the police?"

"I'm going to hold a press conference. This evening. I'll tell the world what I've done and why, and I'll take whatever consequences come my way."

"That's admirable. But what about Max? And what about us?"

"I know," Bea said. "It's scary. But I have to do it. I won't be able to live with myself if I don't. And besides, the person behind the video seems to know the truth, anyway. There's no hiding from him or her. I won't lie or deny the truth."

"Okay," Travis said reluctantly. "The thought of losing you the same day I got you back is downright heartbreaking. But like I said, I love and support you, no matter what. If you say this is what we're doing, then this is what we're doing."

"Thank you, babe," Bea said to Travis, calling him babe again for the first time. He smiled back in return.

"So, how can I help?"

"For starters, you can stand by my side when I speak this evening. Will you do that?"

"Yes. Done."

"You can also help notify the press. I want as many TV news and print outlets there as possible. I want to get out in front of this thing. Besides, I figure the more media representatives there are in attendance, the more likely they are to report the story fairly."

"Good point," Travis agreed. "How about Max? Do you want him to be there?"

"I do," Bea replied. "In fact, I'd like to go back to the house and talk with Max as soon as we're done eating. I'd like to tell him everything, including that you and I are together now."

"Wow," Travis said. "Are you sure?"

"I certainly am. I'm as sure as I was when you asked me in Galley Books this morning if I was sure about... You know," Bea added, making them both blush.

Suddenly, Bea noticed a familiar man walking towards them. He was dressed in old jeans and a t-shirt, with a flannel left unbuttoned over top. It took her a minute to realize who he was.

"Kyle?" she said, remembering now. "Kyle... Hodges, right?"

He acted surprised to see Bea, but the reaction didn't seem genuine. For a second, she wondered if Kyle had followed her here. She quickly dismissed the idea, thinking that wasn't possible since she was driving Gabby's car. But something unusual was going on. Bea could feel it.

"What a surprise, Beatrice!" he replied, bowing towards her in a stifled, phony pose. "Who's your friend?"

Bea swallowed hard. This was the first of many moments of truth she would have to face in the coming days. All her talk about honesty would mean nothing if her actions weren't in line with her speech. She thought about introducing Travis as her boyfriend. Or significant other.

Did thirty-something adults call each other boyfriend and girlfriend?

But John and Max didn't know yet, and she owed it to them to let them hear the news first.

"This is Travis Earl," Bea said without describing her

relationship to him. "Travis, meet Kyle Hodges. He's a colleague of John's."

Travis extended a hand to shake Kyle's. Bea was again struck by how strong and handsome Travis looked compared to John and his fellow office-worker types. "Pleased to meet you," Travis said politely.

"Does your husband know you and Travis are here together? And that you've taken off your wedding ring?" Kyle asked with a serious expression on his face.

Bea could see Travis tense up. She hadn't told him about last night at Honey Hog, so he didn't know she already thought Kyle was strange. He was getting that idea on his own.

"Kyle, it was great to meet you," Travis said, standing up out of the booth and flexing his muscles like he had done in the school office with John. He positioned himself in between Kyle and Bea. "If you don't mind, we'd like to get back to our lunch. It looks like our waitress has our food ready. You have a good day now."

Kyle raised his eyebrows and looked shocked as Kai arrived at the table. She sat Bea and Travis' plates down in what turned out to be perfect timing. Kyle huffed, then turned on his heel like a soldier doing an about face. He walked out of the diner, letting the door slam behind him.

"Sorry about that," Bea said, forgetting that she didn't have to apologize around Travis.

"You don't have to…"

"I know. Let me rephrase. That guy is weird. I appreciate you getting rid of him. I have to admit, it's hot when you stand up and flex all of your muscles like that. You make every other man feel physically inferior. And

I'm the lucky lady who gets to feel those muscles up close and personal."

"I don't know about all that," Travis said as he took a gulp of tea and slathered some mayonnaise on his sandwich. "I'm not trying to make other men feel inferior. Not trying to show my physical dominance or anything."

"You mean *lesser* men," Bea added with a smile.

"If you say so. But you know I'd lay down my life for you, right?"

"Wow," Bea said. "Talk about heavy."

"Oh, that didn't come out quite as slow as I would have liked. I mean… I guess I could have built up to that a little better."

Bea reached across the table for Travis' hand. She didn't care who might notice. "I hear you. And it's sweet. I really do love the way you adore me."

They both smiled as they ate their lunch and talked. The interaction between them was effortless. And the attraction remained intense. Bea found herself thinking about when they would make love again. It was better than thinking about being arrested, she reasoned.

When they were finished at the diner, Bea and Travis sat in Gabby's parked car and got on their mobile phones to spread the word about the evening press conference. Bea messaged her sisters, Gabby, and her mom to invite them all to attend. She asked that Lana wait to tell Max until Bea could be there to do it herself, but she wanted her mom to have a heads up since the event had the potential to be momentous. Travis made calls to the media, and he made arrangements for the event to take place outside of town hall. No special permission was needed to assemble in the public square, but he let town officials know as a courtesy.

"How about John?" Travis asked. "He has a right to know."

As if on cue, Bea's phone rang. She recognized the number as her husband's.

"Hello?" Bea said as she answered.

"Another video has been released. I thought you'd like to know," John said. "This one may be substantially more upsetting to you than the last. I'm sorry." Then he hung up the phone. They were beyond cordial greetings and unnecessary words.

37

Whan Bea and Travis arrived at the Hughes house, the reporters from the morning were nowhere to be found. John's SUV was gone. As Bea parked Gabby's car and they walked towards the back patio, she saw that Myra White was sitting outside with Lana.

"Bea!" Myra said. "You're just the person I was hoping to see."

"Is that so?" Bea asked as she walked over to give her neighbor a polite hug. "Let me first introduce you and Mom to my friend, Travis."

Lana looked thrilled to finally meet Travis. "I've heard so much about you, Travis. Welcome," she said.

"The same goes for you, Mrs. Denton, ma'am," Travis said as he took Lana's hand and gently kissed the top of it. "Now I see where Bea gets her good looks."

Lana blushed. Travis had already won her over.

Bea didn't want to be rude to Myra, but she needed to talk to her mom and her son. Time was passing quickly, and the day was getting away from her. "Myra, what can I do for you, my friend?" Bea asked, hoping to speed whatever it was along.

Myra hesitated. She looked from Bea to Travis a few times, then over to Lana. "You know what?" she asked. "I have a roast in the oven that I should really go back home and tend to. We can talk another time."

"Okay," Bea said. "If you don't mind, that would probably be best for me, too." Bea looked at her mother, who gave her a wink, letting Bea know she approved of having Myra wait until another time.

"Then it's settled," Myra said. "We'll catch up another time soon." She said goodbye and walked across the grass towards her home.

"Now," Bea said when Myra was past the line of trees in the side yard and out of earshot. "Mom, I need to have a serious discussion with you and Max. Right away. Will you come inside?"

Travis stood dutifully at Bea's side. He smiled at Lana, looking patient, but eager to get the show on the road at the same time.

"Absolutely," Lana replied. "If this is about what I think it is, then I'm looking forward to it."

Bea smiled at her mom, and they all walked inside.

When they arrived indoors, Max was upstairs in his room. "How has he been today?" Bea asked her mom before calling him down.

"He seems a little worried, but mostly okay." Lana replied. "He's been busy playing video games." She tilted her head towards Travis. "Does he know?"

"He knows everything," Bea said as Travis shook his

head in agreement. "And I haven't scared him off yet," Bea added with a laugh.

"No place I'd rather be," Travis said as he wrapped one arm around Bea's shoulders. Lana smiled as she saw it happen. She wanted her daughter to be loved like that.

Bea knew there were a lot of logistics to sort out. Even if she managed to avoid being arrested after tonight's public confession, she would need to find a new place to live. That went for Max and Lana, too. It wouldn't feel right to stay in John's home. Bea wanted a fresh start in a home where she knew she could relax and make positive memories. She hated that she'd have to uproot her mom and son, but she knew it would be for the best long-term. Natalie's offer to have Lana stay with her in Sacramento still stood. The family would need to get together and discuss options.

"Max?" Bea called up the stairs. "Can you come down here for a minute?"

It took Max less than a minute to run downstairs. He was eager to find out what was happening. He didn't like waiting around for information any more than Bea did. When he entered the kitchen and saw Travis, his eyes lit up with recognition. It thrilled Bea to see it happen. She would never push Travis on Max, but she hoped that a good relationship would develop between them naturally.

"Hey, Max," Travis said cheerfully, reaching one arm out to give the boy a fist bump. It was just the kind of guy-to-guy camaraderie Bea had hoped to see.

"Hey Travis," Max replied, lifting his fist up for the bump.

"You remembered my name. Awesome."

"Yeah," Max confirmed. "What are you doing here?"

Bea stepped in. "I invited him," she explained. "I need to have an important talk with you and Grandma. And I want Travis here while I do. How about we sit down at the table to have our talk?"

"Okay," Max said. Bea thought he seemed curious, but cooperative.

Bea directed Travis to the dining room table where they all took a seat. It felt like a full-circle moment, because Bea had met Travis for the first time when she visited his furniture shop to pick out this very table. It seemed fitting that she would tell her mother and son she and Travis were together now as they all sat around this very special table. Bea made a mental note to tell John she wanted to take the table with her when she moved out. She didn't figure he'd mind. After all, why would he want reminded of the day his wife met the man she would leave him for?

"So, what do you want to tell us?" Max asked, his bright eyes eager to learn whatever it was his mom had to say. "Is it about Dad? Is it his temper again?"

"No, that's not it," Bea said. "At least, that's not all."

"Go ahead," Lana prompted her daughter. "We're listening."

Bea took a slow, deep breath and looked up at the ceiling. She knew the words she was about to speak would change their lives forever. When she told Max what she had done, he might never look at her the same way. When she told Max she was leaving his dad and seeing Travis, he might not look at her the same way. But both truths had to be told. There was no turning back now. Bea could only hope her son would understand why. She hoped that if not now, someday he could have compassion for everything she'd been through. She hoped her son would believe she'd done her best for him.

"Max, I have two things to tell you, and they're big. I'm not sure which one is the easiest to talk about, so I'll start with the reason Travis is here."

"Okay."

"Your father and I are getting a divorce," Bea blurted. She leaned back in her chair and put her palms flat on the table as she waited for Max's response. He looked at her, stunned. He didn't speak. No one did. After a long few minutes had passed, Bea tried again. "Did you hear what I said, son? Your dad and I are getting a divorce. We're... Separating."

"I heard you," Max said. "Like the reporter said this morning. They were right. And Travis is going to be your boyfriend."

"Yes," Bea confirmed, swallowing hard. The conversation was turning out to be more difficult than she'd realized.

"Why?"

"That's a very long story," Bea replied. "The important thing to know is that your dad and I care about each other. We will still be friends. And we both love you very much. That will never change."

"I mean, why do you have a boyfriend already?"

"Max," Lana inserted. "Hear your mom out. It's understandable that you're upset, but I promise you she's doing what she thinks is best."

Travis reached under the table and squeezed Bea's

hand. The warmth of his skin felt so good. She was happy to be part of a couple. A real couple.

"Travis and I have known each other ever since you were a baby," Bea explained. "The truth is, Max, your dad and I have always been better friends than we have been a married couple. I'm not sure why that is, but I knew something was different not long after our wedding. By the time you were born a year later, I was sure. And then, when you were a baby and we were shopping for furniture, I met Travis."

"Has he been your boyfriend since I was a baby?"

"No," Bea said. "But I've known I wanted him to be. I stayed with your dad to give it my very best try. I wanted us to be a happy family."

"But we're not."

"Right," Bea confirmed. "We love each other. That's for sure. But I now understand that me, you, and your dad will be a better family and a happier family if he and I aren't married."

Max sat quietly as he fiddled with the edge of a cloth napkin on the tabletop. Bea let him have his time and space to think. She waited for him to ask questions when he was ready.

"Are we going to move to a new house?"

"Yes," Bea confirmed. "We are. I'm not sure where your dad will live. Maybe he'll stay living in this house. But I'll live in a different house, probably with your grandma. And you'll have two homes. One with me and one with your dad. As far as I'm concerned, you can go back and forth anytime you want. I want it to be comfortable. I imagine your dad will say the same."

"I know how it works," Max said. "I have friends at school whose parents are divorced and they have two houses. Some of them have stepmoms and stepdads."

Bea reached her free hand across the table and took her son's. "I know that all sounds scary. It's a little scary for me, too. Change usually is. But we will get through it together. You'll see. Your dad and I will both be happier, and that will be good for us all."

Travis cleared his throat. It startled even him. He wasn't intending to interject, but he was nervous.

"Will we live with him?" Max asked, gesturing towards Travis.

It was a reasonable question. Bea wasn't sure how to answer yet. She'd made enough decisions for one day and wasn't ready to make any more.

"I'm not sure yet," she answered, truthfully. "But when I figure it out, you'll be the first to know. Does that sound fair?"

"Sounds fair to me," Lana said, trying to be encouraging. She reached over and tousled some of Max's hair. "I'll be with you every step of the way, grandson. It won't be so bad, I promise."

Max sighed begrudgingly. Bea could tell he wanted to cooperate. He was just trying to wrap his mind around it. "I guess it's fair, yeah." He also seemed like he had something to say.

"Is there something you need to tell us?" Bea asked.

Max hesitated for a long minute, moving his fingers quickly back and forth across the cloth napkin. "I guess... Not right now." He looked at Travis as he said it. Max wasn't ready to share with him.

"Okay, for now," Bea confirmed. "We'll keep going to the next part."

"Yeah, what's the second thing you need to say?" Max asked.

Bea took the biggest, deepest breath ever, then she told Max what had happened at Eagle's Point. She told him how the person on the videos was right and how she might be arrested. She told him how the wretched man had locked him in the bathroom and was trying to take him away. She told him she'd hit the man with a baseball bat and then pushed him over the edge. And she told him she was going to make a public confession. When she finished, Max said but one simple sentence in response.

"Mom, you're the very best."

38

T he size of the crowd surprised Bea as she gazed out the window of the stately Town Hall lobby. Folding chairs were assembled in front of the podium where she was to speak outdoors on the square. Already, there was standing room only. Her family was sitting on the front row to show their support. Max, Lana, Natalie, Ruth, and Ruth's husband Steve waited patiently. Bea didn't see Gabby, but she assumed an empty seat next to Max was being saved for her. Word of the press conference had apparently spread quickly, because Myra White, Jenny McGuire, Annie Rogers, and Susana Herrera sat amongst the crowd. Reporters and cameramen gathered at the back, testing their equipment and periodically filming briefings in advance of the event.

Bea had left a voicemail for John to warn him about her public confession, but she wasn't sure whether he'd received it. She figured a member of his staff would have brought it to his attention by now as well. His office was in the same building where she was waiting. She knew what she was about to do would change John's life. But it had to happen. Her resolve was strong.

Travis sat in a wingback chair beside Bea, holding her hand as she stood. He was dressed in nice pants and a blue and white button-down shirt with a navy sport coat. Bea had never seen him dressed so nicely. She thought he looked even more handsome than usual. Maybe it was because her mind drifted to special occasions they'd attend together in the future. Seeing Travis dress the part made those events seem more real. More within reach. Maybe, Bea would exhibit at an art gallery again one day. Travis would dress up and attend her shows, showering her with praise and warm kisses.

Bea had purposely stayed off the internet all afternoon. She knew another video had been released thanks to John's call, but she had decided not to watch it. She figured it wouldn't change what she would say, anyway, and she wanted her head clear when she spoke. Travis supported her decision. He'd turned his phone off in a show of support. Neither of them knew what the rumor mill was churning out next. And they liked it that way.

"Hey, babe," Travis began, standing up. "I'm going to stop by the restroom before we get started. We have about fifteen minutes until go time, right?"

Bea looked at the clock on the wall. "Yeah, about that. I'll go with you. I could stand to splash some cold water on my face."

"Do you think they have one of those unisex rooms we can go into together?" Travis asked, only half joking.

Bea smiled. She always had fun with Travis. He had a way of making things easier to bear. She looked forward to his happy presence in her life. "You're too much," she said with a chuckle as they walked hand-in-hand out of the lobby and down a long hall, looking for the restroom. "We only have fifteen minutes."

"Based on the time we clocked this morning, I don't think that will be a problem."

Bea blushed and slogged Travis on the arm, teasing.

"Ouch, you brute," he joked as they came upon the very sort of unisex restroom Travis was referring to. John's office was on the other side of the building, and Bea didn't think she'd ever been on this side. She was unfamiliar with the layout. "Hey, here it is," Travis said. "Let's go in."

Bea paused, thinking about how little time they had. But she wanted Travis again. She quickly acquiesced "Okay," she said. "After you."

Taking the lead, Travis leaned with his weight and opened the door, one hand still intertwined with Bea's. The door latch caught at first, like maybe it had been locked, but the force of Travis' push had jimmied it. Unencumbered by the latch, the door burst open, swinging wide on its hinges. As it opened fully, Bea and Travis saw a sight they never would have expected. The small space was filled with two men, naked and sweaty in a compromising position. Both men kept their eyes closed at first. They were too immersed in their lovemaking to notice the onlookers at the door. Heaving and thrusting vigorously and clearly enjoying himself, the man on top finally slowed to a stop as he glanced up and a look of horror spread across his face.

"*Beatrice*?"

"My God, John," she replied, covering her mouth with one hand. "And... Kyle."

39

I*t all makes sense*, Bea thought to herself as Travis shut the door, giving John and Kyle their privacy.

"Babe," Travis said, looking deeply into Bea's eyes to see how she was taking the revelation. "Are you okay?"

Bea stumbled backwards, leaning against a wall in the hallway as she struggled to get her bearings. The lack of romance, the friend-like rapport, and John's building frustration with their marriage all fit like a puzzle, suddenly complete with the insertion of one final, missing piece. "I am," Bea said. "I truly am. It was never about me. It wasn't my fault! But wow. I can't believe I missed this."

John rushed into the hallway, frantically piecing his clothing together. "Beatrice, I'm so sorry. I really am." He sounded more sincere than he had in ages. "I don't know what to say. I'm so, so sorry."

Travis stepped back, while Bea stepped forward. Tears began to stream down her cheeks. "It's fine," she said.

stepping closer to John and taking his face in her hands. "John, it's *fine*. I didn't know…"

John began to cry now, big, fat tears. "I couldn't tell you," he said between sobs. "I'm… I mean, I'm… Well…"

"You're gay."

John nodded his head up and down to confirm, Bea's hands wiping his tears as her own continued to fall. "Yes." He leaned his head down on his wife's shoulder as he cried. She cradled him, wrapping her arms tightly around his shoulders and rocking him back and forth.

"John Hughes, don't you be sorry," she said through her own tears. "This is who you are. You said I couldn't understand you. But now I do."

"Oh, Bea," John said. It was the first time she could remember that he'd called her by the name she preferred. Suddenly, he didn't seem like a condescending father figure. Suddenly, he seemed like a cherished friend. She loved this man. And now they could love each other properly, as dear friends and co-parents to a wonderful boy.

Kyle emerged from the bathroom, more put together than John, but still disheveled. He looked at John and Bea embracing each other and was unsure of what to do or say. His demeanor was different than it had been at Honey Hog and Lorraine's. His adversarial air was gone.

"He's…" John began. "Kyle is my…"

"He's your love," Bea said, finishing her husband's sentence. "I get it."

"Oh, Bea," John said again, crying like a baby now.

"Shh," she said as she pressed her husband's head

against her shoulder and continued to rock him. "I've got you. We're okay. We're all okay."

Travis stepped towards Kyle and extended a hand. "Kyle, man, I'm sorry I was short with you earlier. I didn't know…"

"No problem," Kyle said, shaking Travis' hand. "We're good." Even his voice was different than it had been before. He sounded calm and relaxed, without pretense.

"You called it, man," Travis continued. "Bea and I are together, and John didn't know." Travis turned to John and Bea, who then turned to face their lovers. "John, I owe you the truth," Travis added. "I love Bea with all my heart. We're beginning a life together. And I hope that you and I can be friends."

"Yes, I'd like that, too," John said. "Here I suspected you were the person behind the videos. I was wrong. I'm sorry. I'm glad we all know the truth now."

"Wait," Bea interjected. "What do you mean about the videos? Do you know who is behind them?"

"Oh, you don't?" John mumbled, looking nervously at Kyle.

"No," Bea said, confused. "We've had our phones off all afternoon. I wanted a clear head before my statement. We haven't seen the last video or any news about it. So, please fill us in."

John looked up at the ceiling, muttering. He didn't seem to want to say it.

"It was me," Kyle blurted. "I was jealous."

"Wow," Bea said.

"I know. I've loved John for a long time. I wanted him

to leave you so we could be together, and he was always too wrapped up in his public image to do so. He didn't think he could remain mayor if he left his wife and came out as gay."

"I know how that goes," Bea said, cracking a smile. "The public image part, anyway."

"I guess you do," Kyle replied. "It wasn't my finest hour. But John had told me what happened at Eagle's Point. I was so desperate for him to leave you and the office of mayor so we could be together that I hatched this plan to ensure I'd get him all to myself. It was the only way I could come up with. I'm sorry, Bea. I was desperate."

"Wow," Bea said again. It was hard to find other words.

"I'm resigning," John said. "I drafted the letter this afternoon and submitted it less than an hour ago. If you don't mind me crashing your press conference, I'll announce my resignation to the public."

"Are you certain you want to do that?" Bea asked. "I know how important your job is to you."

"I am," John said. "Kyle and I are in love. He deserves a partner who will put him first. No job is more important than that."

Bea smiled and looked over at Travis. She was happy that John got it. Finally. He was becoming a better man, and it made her proud. "Then I wish the two of you all the best," she said.

The four of them chatted for a few more minutes, happy and relieved to have everything out in the open between them. Bea could tell that they would all get along well, and that they'd make a great group of parental figures for Max. All was well that ends well.

"I hate to break up this party," Travis said. "But, babe, you had better get out there. It's time."

"You're right," Bea said. "I've got to face the music."

"I'm right beside you," Travis said.

"Me, too," John echoed. "Let's do this."

Before they could turn to walk back to the front of the building, they heard a woman's voice shouting.

"Wait!" she yelled. "Please! Wait!" Bea wondered if it was another reporter angling for a private interview until she recognized the woman's voice.

"Gabby!" Bea shouted as her friend rounded the corner and came into view. "What are you doing in here? I'm about to go out there and confess."

"You will do no such thing," she said as she flung open her leather satchel and pulled out a manila file folder. "And hello, everyone," she said, looking at Travis and Kyle. "I'm not sure who you two are or what is happening here, but we'll have time for introductions later."

Travis and Kyle nodded their understanding.

"What?" Bea pleaded.

"I have the best news for you. And I do mean the *best.*"

"Okay, get on with it, Gab," Bea said.

"I've just come from the Norcal Federal Prison near Sacramento. I found the guy. It's all documented right here. He didn't die!" A hush fell over the four of them as they listened, in complete and total shock. "He didn't die, Bea. He didn't die. You didn't kill anyone."

"But how…" Bea asked. "I hit him with a baseball bat and pushed him over… I saw…"

"I don't know all the details, but he's alive. And he's a very bad man."

"My God," John mumbled.

"The injury you gave him caused him to seek treatment at a clinic, and that's how he was apprehended. A young nurse who said the man gave her the willies convinced her supervisors to check into his record," Gabby explained, her voice somber. "His DNA matched that found on the bodies of two young children who were kidnapped in Marin County. They washed up in San Francisco."

Bea thought she might vomit. She was revolted by the vile man's actions. Two babies, taken away from their families... and *killed*. "My Max... My God..." Bea muttered. "How sick."

"I know," Gabby said. "I spoke with the warden. It was all I could do to get through the meeting without hurling into his trash can. It's sickening. But you know what this means?"

"I do. She's a hero," Travis proclaimed. "That's my girl." He leaned over and kissed Bea lightly on the lips. "I'm so proud of you, babe."

"Exactly!" Gabby said, jumping up and down. "And now I know who this one is. Travis Earl, huh?"

"Pleased to meet you, Gabby," he replied with a smile.

"John's gay, we're divorcing and will remain friends, and this is his partner, Kyle," Bea added, gesturing. "Now you're all caught up."

They all laughed. It felt good.

EPILOGUE

B ea canceled the press conference, noting that the claims in the video had been debunked and that she had no additional comment. Instead, she reserved a table for ten at Honey Hog where her big, happy family enjoyed a nice dinner together without incident.

John gave the people of Rosemary Run the chance to prove that they could accept his relationship with Kyle and amicable divorce from Bea while he remained in the office of mayor. He tore up his letter of resignation just in time and was pleasantly surprised when they did exactly that.

Bea and Travis followed by John and Kyle had beautiful, meaningful wedding ceremonies with receptions where they all danced until dawn. Assisted by Ruth's real estate firm and Natalie's title company, the couples found new homes just down the street from each other where Max can go back and forth as he pleased. Max positively blossomed under the love and protection of so many happy people, eventually deciding to attend art school like his mother.

Explaining that Freddy Denton had left money for just such an occasion, Lana paid cash for a building downtown to house her daughter's new art gallery. Ruth and Natalie threw Bea a fabulous party to celebrate the grand opening. Now, Bea regularly hosts events so popular with townspeople and tourists alike that there is typically standing room only as crowds clamor to purchase her works of art.

The painting Bea created of the old couple on the bench hangs in a prominent spot in her gallery, reminding her every day of the beauty that lies in growing and changing, and the irreplaceable worth of a dear, treasured friend.

————

Get the next book in the series:

Her Boldest Lie
Rosemary Run - Book Three
kellyutt.com

ENJOY THIS BOOK?

A NOTE FROM AUTHOR KELLY UTT

Did you enjoy this book? You can make a big difference.

Reviews are the most powerful tools in my arsenal when it comes to getting attention for my books. As much as I'd like to, I don't have the financial muscle of a New York publisher. I can't take out full page ads in the newspaper or put posters on the subway.

(Not yet, anyway.)

But I do have something much more effective than that, and it's something that those publishers would kill to get their hands on.

A committed and loyal group of readers.

Honest reviews of my books help bring them to the attention of other readers.

If you've enjoyed this book, I would be very grateful if you could spend just five minutes leaving a review (it can be as short as you like) on the book's Amazon page and on Goodreads or BookBub.

Thank you very much.

ALSO BY KELLY UTT

Have you read them all?

———

In the Rosemary Run Series

In the charming Northern California town of Rosemary Run, there's trouble brewing below the picture-perfect surface. Don't let the manicured lawns and stylish place settings fool you. Nothing is exactly as it seems. Secrets and lies threaten to upend the status quo and destroy lives when— not if— they're revealed.

BOOK 1 - HER DEEPEST FEAR

BOOK 2 - HER HIDDEN PAST

BOOK 3 - HER BOLDEST LIE

BOOK 4 - HER DARKEST HOUR

BOOK 5 - HER BURIED SECRET

BOOK 6 - HER WORST MISTAKE

———

In The Past Life Series

The Past Life Series chronicles the Hartmann and Davies families across time and space. This life-affirming story, anchored by the deep affection between George and Alessandra, reveals how the connections we share can ground us during even the most difficult times as we endeavor to learn what we're made of.

Join the family you'll feel like you already know as, together, they explore the meaning of life beyond what lies on the surface and fight to keep each other safe.

SHORT STORY PREQUEL - WAIT FOR OUR TURN

BOOK 1 - TELL ME I'M SAFE

BOOK 2 - SHOW ME THE DANGER

BOOK 3 - KEEP THEM FROM HARM

BOOK 4 - TAKE ME TO FIGHT

BOOK 5 - PICK UP THE PIECES

———

Be the first to know when new books are released by signing up for Kelly's e-mail list at www.kellyutt.com.

Kindle Unlimited Subscribers read for free.

ABOUT THE AUTHOR

STANDARDS OF STARLIGHT BOOKS
KELLY UTT

Kelly Utt writes emotional novels for readers who enjoy both suspense and sentimentality. She was born in Youngstown, Ohio in 1976.

Kelly grew up with a dad who would read a book on a weighty topic, ask her to read it, too, and then insist they discuss it together, igniting her passion for life's big questions. That passion is often reflected inKelly's novels, giving them a depth which leaves readers wanting more and thinking about her stories long after the last lines are read.

Kelly holds a Bachelor's degree in psychology from the

University of Tennessee, Knoxville and she studied graduate-level interactive media at Quinnipiac University.

She lives in the Nashville suburb of Franklin, Tennessee with her husband and sons.

www.kellyutt.com